Heartbeat in the Hall

When Desire Meets the Pulse of Danger

Trevor Jensen

Dedication

For those who've stood in silent corridors, fighting invisible battles with steady hands and tired hearts—

This story is for you.

For the healers who carry hope like a scalpel, carving light into the darkest hours—

This story is for you.

And for anyone who has ever risked love after loss, trusted again after betrayal,or dared to believe that some hearts are meant to find their way back—

This story is especially for you.

— Trevor Jensen

Contents

Introduction

The first time Dr. Emily Carter felt her heart race uncontrollably, it wasn't in the ER.

It was the moment she saw Lucas Hayes again.

She'd stitched together shattered bones, braced through cardiac arrests, and held the hands of strangers as life slipped quietly away. But nothing prepared her for what it would feel like to have her carefully constructed world torn open—not by trauma or tragedy, but by the return of a man who once made her believe in forever.

Now, in the storm-lit hallways of St. Theresa's Hospital, secrets lurk behind polished name badges and sterile gloves. Patients vanish, data is buried, and someone is watching her every move. As Emily searches for her missing sister, she's pulled into a shadowy conspiracy where trust is dangerous, and love could be lethal.

Lucas is no longer the reckless med student who once kissed her in the on-call room. He's a trauma surgeon with a reputation for breaking rules—and hearts. But he also holds pieces of the puzzle Emily can't ignore. And when the whispers in the halls grow louder, when threats turn physical and no one else can be trusted, the only safe place might be back in his arms.

Heartbeat in the Halls is a slow-burn romantic thriller pulsing with emotional depth, high-stakes suspense, and the undeniable electricity of a second chance. For readers who believe that healing isn't just about medicine—but about risking everything for the people you love.

Your heart may pound. It may even ache.

But it will never beat the same again.

Chapter 1 - Crash Cart Emotions

*S*t. *Theresa's Hospital, 6:03 a.m. – Storm overhead. Heartbeats everywhere.*

The shrill wail of the ambulance bay doors cracked open and sliced through the fog-drenched dawn, chasing thunder into the gleaming linoleum corridors of St. Theresa's ER. Dr. Emily Carter didn't flinch. Her gloved hands moved with practiced precision as she pressed gauze against a jagged chest wound.

"Vitals crashing," a nurse called out over the noise.

"Push two more of epi. Charge the paddles—now," Emily instructed, her voice level. Her hazel eyes, always sharp, stayed locked on the monitor. The boy's heart rate was flickering—erratic, fading.

The trauma team moved like a synchronized current around her, every step rehearsed, efficient. But the chill creeping into Emily's chest had nothing to do with the room temperature. A heartbeat faltered. Her fingers froze.

Suddenly, she was back in that other room—scrubbing her hands raw, soap stinging her skin. A child's voice echoing in her ears. *"Will it hurt, Dr. Carter?"* Then silence. Little Lily's hand had slipped from hers before the ambulance even left the bay.

Not now.

She blinked hard and refocused.

"Clear!" she called.

The patient's chest jumped as the charge jolted through him. For a heartbeat, time stopped.

Then the monitor lit up. A slow, steady rhythm.

"Got it," the nurse confirmed, relief palpable.

"Stabilize and prep for CT," Emily said. "Keep that dressing tight."

As the gurney rolled out, Emily leaned back against the wall, breath steadying, her stethoscope warm against her neck. Her fingers, still gloved, trembled. She shoved them into her coat pockets.

"You're still the rock," came a familiar voice beside her.

Patty Moreno, night shift nurse and part-time ER therapist, gave her a crooked grin. "Storm outside, storm inside—and there you are, calm in the middle like some kind of Zen trauma goddess."

Emily exhaled through a smile. "Blinking wastes time."

"Right. And feelings are for amateurs."

Emily shrugged, but didn't respond. The overhead lights flickered with the storm. Then came the next shift in energy. A quiet ripple through the ER.

The doors whooshed open.

He walked in like he owned the chaos—tall, rain-drenched, trauma bag slung across his shoulder. His sandy hair was soaked to the roots, jaw rough with stubble. His eyes scanned the room, calculating, unfazed.

Lucas Hayes.

The name had buzzed through the hospital halls like an errant EKG all week. Transferred early. Some whispered scandal. And now, mid-storm, mid-crisis, he was here—unannounced and dripping onto the tiles.

"Where's the subdural bleed?" he asked the nearest nurse, not breaking stride.

"Trauma Bay Three," she stammered.

Emily stepped forward. "He's not cleared. No onboarding, no access privileges."

"I don't need a badge to keep a kid from dying," Lucas replied, already disappearing into the trauma bay.

She didn't have time to argue. She followed.

Inside, a teen lay motionless, his skull visibly fractured. Monitors shrieked. The attending was prepping for transfer to OR.

Lucas hovered, eyes locked on the cranial pressure readout.

"No time," he said. "We do this here. Burr hole. Now."

"You're not cleared to touch him," Emily snapped.

"He's herniating. Sixty seconds and we lose him. Help me or report me. Your call."

Emily hesitated—just long enough to curse herself—then grabbed the drill kit.

Together, in sterile silence broken only by alarms, they worked. Lucas made the incision, Emily suctioned. Blood spattered the tray. Then a slow, cathartic hiss of pressure release.

Monitors began to settle.

The boy's color returned. Nurses exhaled. One clapped Lucas on the back.

Emily peeled off her gloves with a snap.

Outside, Patty leaned on a gurney with raised brows.

"Well, hell," she said. "Looks like the hurricane met the lightning bolt."

An hour later, Emily stood in front of the stainless steel dispenser in the staff lounge, trying to pin her curls back into a semblance of order. Her zebra-striped socks peeked from under scrubs soaked at the hems.

Lucas leaned against the far counter, sipping something dark from a battered thermos. Cinnamon laced the air.

"Just so we're clear," Emily said, not turning around, "you made five policy violations in ten minutes."

"Six, if you count walking in through the ambulance bay," Lucas replied, casual.

She glanced at him, expression neutral. "We follow rules for a reason."

"Patients bleed whether or not there's red tape."

"Rules keep people alive."

Lucas's eyes met hers, steady. "So does instinct."

Emily crossed her arms. "You're not the only one with it."

"I noticed," he said, not quite smiling.

She blinked, thrown for just a second. Then turned to the fruit bowl. The apples were low again.

"You eat apples during charting?" Lucas asked.

"They help me focus."

"Huh. Functional snacking. I like it."

Patty burst into the room with her usual whirlwind energy. "Oh good, both of you in one place. Should I alert HR, or will the fire alarm go off on its own?"

"Not today," Emily said, reaching for a clipboard.

Patty leaned closer to Lucas, grinning. "You know, she warms up. Eventually. You just need a defibrillator for her heart."

"I'm not looking to warm anything," Lucas muttered.

"Mm-hmm." Patty turned to Emily. "Also, you should know—after that little drama in Bay Three? He asked about you."

Emily's spine straightened. "What?"

"Not in a flirty way. In a... loaded way. Said, 'What happened to Dr. Carter?' Like he already knew something bad had happened and wanted confirmation."

Emily forced her tone flat. "He doesn't know anything."

Patty's eyes twinkled. "Not yet."

Emily moved through the administrative wing with her eyes down, heart still pounding. She reached the trauma board and froze. Her name had just been updated—paired with Lucas Hayes for the rest of the day's incoming traumas.

Perfect.

"Coincidence?" came a voice behind her.

She turned. Dr. Jasmine Rao, Chief of Trauma, watched her like a hawk appraising flight.

"I don't believe in coincidences," Emily said.

"Good. Because I assigned you."

Emily raised a brow. "Based on... punishment?"

"Based on results. He's on probation. You're the best litmus test."

"I'm not a babysitter."

"No. You're an applicant for Head of Trauma. Which means I expect leadership. And emotional composure."

Emily hesitated. "Lucas is reckless."

"Reckless saved a life an hour ago," Jasmine said. "You of all people should know that sometimes rules need to bend to serve the outcome."

Emily didn't respond.

Jasmine added more softly, "Don't let ghosts keep you from leading the living."

The PA crackled: "Incoming trauma—multi-vehicle accident, three patients enroute."

Jasmine nodded toward the trauma bay. "This one's big. Show me what two of my best can do."

Emily stood in Bay Five as the trauma team assembled. The air vibrated with readiness. Outside, the storm drummed against windows like impatient fingers.

Lucas joined her, already gloved up.

"We doing this?" he asked.

She glanced at him. He looked calm. Centered.

"No bulldozers," she said.

He almost smiled. "Just us, then."

For a split second, something stirred in her. Not fear. Not adrenaline. Something else.

Her pulse skipped.

Hope? Or danger wearing a stethoscope?

The bay doors burst open, and the gurneys rolled in.

Time to find out.

Chapter 2 - The Sins of the Past

Hospital Staff Lounge, Midday – Fluorescent lights, murmurs, and lingering rumors fill the air.

The staff lounge buzzed with barely contained tension, hushed voices bouncing off beige walls and flickering fluorescent lights. The clatter of spoons in coffee mugs masked just enough of the murmurs to make them feel like secrets.

Emily Carter sat near the window, her half-eaten sandwich ignored on the table. A cold cup of coffee hovered at her elbow, untouched. Her body was still buzzing from the earlier trauma cases, but her mind kept slipping—to Lily, to Lucas, to the competing voices inside her.

Across the room, a knot of nurses huddled by the vending machine.

"You saw what he did, right?" one said, leaning in. "Lucas Hayes. Straight-up cowboyed that procedure. Didn't even have clearance."

"He pulled it off, though," said another. "That burr hole probably saved the kid."

A third voice dropped to a whisper. "Yeah, well, that's what got him into trouble at Greystone. I heard he intubated a peds patient solo—without backup, no supervisor. Kid coded. Barely made it. Parents almost sued the hospital."

Emily kept her gaze on her phone screen, pretending to scroll through patient logs. She wasn't listening, not really. Except she was. Every word sliced deeper than she expected.

"His name was all over the board review," someone else added. "He left before the investigation was closed. That's what I heard."

Lucas sat at the far edge of the lounge, silent, shoulders slightly hunched as if absorbing every barb. He didn't react, but his grip on his mug tightened.

Emily watched him out of the corner of her eye. He looked calm—too calm. Like someone who'd learned that reacting only fed the fire.

Her phone buzzed. ADMIN CALL – DR. RAO.

She picked up.

"Dr. Carter," Jasmine Rao's voice came through, clipped and cool. "I need you in my office. Now."

"I'm on break—"

"You're also under consideration for Head of Trauma. Priorities."

Emily stood, slipping her phone back into her pocket. As she crossed the lounge, she passed Lucas, whose eyes flicked up—just for a second. They didn't speak.

The hall to Jasmine's office felt colder than usual. Emily paused outside the door, straightened her scrub top, and knocked twice.

"Come."

Inside, Jasmine sat behind her desk, sleeves rolled to the elbow, a file open in front of her.

"I'll be blunt," Jasmine began. "You're one of two remaining finalists for the Trauma Unit leadership position. That comes with visibility—and scrutiny."

Emily nodded slowly. "Understood."

"Good. Because people are talking." Jasmine folded her hands. "About Dr. Hayes. About you. About the possibility that you're... entangled."

Emily bristled. "I've worked two shifts with him."

"You've worked two *very visible* shifts with him. And you defended his field craniotomy in your notes this morning."

Emily's brows drew together. "It saved a life."

"I'm not arguing the outcome," Jasmine said. "But this is a teaching hospital, and optics matter. The wrong perception can sink a good doctor."

There was a pause. Then Jasmine looked away for a beat, her expression flickering.

"Back in my residency," she said quietly, "I vouched for a surgeon who made a mistake. It cost me a fellowship. He moved on. I had to stay and rebuild."

Emily stilled. The admission was unexpected—and raw.

Jasmine leaned forward. "Lucas Hayes might be brilliant. But his past is cloudy, and your future is at stake. Don't confuse compassion for clarity."

Emily left the office more conflicted than when she entered. The hallway lights felt too bright now, the pressure in her chest a little too sharp.

Back in the lounge, she returned just in time to see a young nurse—Jessie, fresh out of school—step toward Lucas with uncertain steps.

"Dr. Hayes," she began, voice tight, "is it true you walked out of an ICU in the middle of a failed airway case? That you left before the kid was stabilized?"

Lucas froze.

Emily stepped closer, not to intervene, just to witness. She saw the way his jaw clenched, the way his fingers curled around the edge of his chair.

"I didn't walk out," he said, voice low but clear. "The team called it before I could fix it. I fought that call. I still hear that kid's monitor when I close my eyes."

The room had gone still.

Jessie blinked. "Sorry. I... I didn't mean to—"

"You meant to ask what kind of doctor I am," Lucas said. "And now you know."

He stood and left the lounge without another word.

Emily exhaled. She hadn't realized she'd been holding her breath.

Later that afternoon, as the skies darkened again outside, Emily met Jasmine's gaze across the trauma board. Another multi-victim trauma alert was flashing red. Lucas's name had been paired with hers—again.

"Problem?" Jasmine asked.

Emily shook her head. "No. Just noting the pattern."

"Good. Because the next call's coming in hot."

Emily moved quickly to the ER bay. Patty fell in beside her, juggling two clipboards and a fresh IV setup.

"You hear what they're saying?" Patty asked, not looking up. "That Lucas left a kid hanging at Greystone? That he covered it up?"

"I heard," Emily said flatly.

Patty glanced sideways. "You believe it?"

"I believe people remember failure more vividly than success. Especially in this place."

"That's not a no."

Emily stopped in front of the trauma bay and turned to her. "I'm not in the business of believing rumors."

"Fair enough." Patty's tone softened. "But whether or not you believe in him, you're tied to him now. People are watching."

"I know."

Patty touched her arm. "So ask yourself—when this gets ugly, what matters more? Your record? Or your gut?"

Emily didn't answer. She didn't have one.

As the first ambulance wheeled in, Emily pulled on gloves, centered herself, and stepped into the fray. Lucas joined her a moment later, wordless but focused. Their movements were seamless—passing tools, making calls, stabilizing vitals like they'd trained together for years.

But under the smooth surface, questions still pulsed.

After the patient was stabilized and wheeled off to the ICU, Emily took a moment in the supply hallway, leaning against the wall, catching her breath.

Lucas appeared beside her, wiping his hands on a sterile towel. "They're not going to stop talking, are they?"

"No," she said. "But that doesn't mean they're right."

He glanced at her. "I didn't expect you to say that."

She shrugged. "Neither did I."

He hesitated, then said, "I don't care what they say. But I care what you think."

The words landed harder than he probably intended.

Emily didn't answer. Instead, she looked down the hall toward the fading echoes of trauma—toward the future they were both trying to rewrite.

Later that evening, as the ER quieted and shift change loomed, Emily sat at the nurses' station reviewing patient notes. Her eyes burned from staring at the screen too long.

Michael texted her: *Coffee? You need it.*

She smiled faintly and started to reply when she noticed something tucked under her tablet. A folded scrap of paper.

She unfolded it.

Typed. Anonymous. Just one sentence:

"Ask him what really happened at Greystone."

Her heart dropped.

She looked up. Across the ER, Lucas stood beside a gurney, laughing gently with a young patient who clung to a stuffed dinosaur. He looked... normal. Compassionate. Human.

But now, the question wasn't whether she believed the rumors.

It was whether he would trust her with the truth.

Outside, the storm rolled back in, darker this time.

Inside, the ER prepared for another night.

And as Emily tucked the note away, her mind echoed with the title that had suddenly taken on a new weight—

The sins of the past don't disappear. They just wait for the right moment to return.

But maybe—just maybe—they weren't the only thing waiting in the dark.

Maybe healing was, too.

Chapter 3 - Synchrnoized Chaos

Trauma Bay, Mid-Afternoon – The air buzzes with alarms, tension, and blood-slick urgency.

"Three incoming," the charge nurse called out, her voice slicing through the electric hum of the trauma bay. "Multi-vehicle accident on Route 9. Two teens and a driver—ETA under five!"

Emily Carter tightened her gloves, pulse surging. The trauma bays were already a symphony of tension—monitors beeping in anticipation, crash carts standing ready, gurneys gleaming under cold light. Even the air felt different. Heavier.

Lucas Hayes was already by her side, sleeves rolled up and jaw set. "Any details?"

"Front seat male, suspected splenic rupture. Back seat—female, unresponsive with shallow breathing. Driver alert but in shock."

Lucas nodded. "We sticking to protocol or going rogue?"

"Let's save them first, argue later," Emily said, scanning the arrival board. "I'll take the boy. You've got the girl."

"Copy that."

The trauma doors slammed open, EMTs wheeling in the first gurney. The boy was limp, pale, and blood soaked through his shirt in dark patches.

"BP's tanking," a medic said. "We've been pushing fluids but he's circling the drain."

"Get him on the monitor. Let's start the FAST scan—now," Emily ordered.

A second gurney followed hard behind, carrying a teenage girl with a cervical collar and glazed eyes.

Lucas leaned in. "Breath rate six. No response to pain. GCS is... maybe six?"

"Should we call anesthesia?" a nurse asked hesitantly, eyes darting to Emily.

Lucas's voice was calm. "No time. I'm intubating."

The nurse blinked. "But—"

"I'll walk you through it later," Lucas said, snapping on sterile gloves. "Suction, please."

Emily didn't argue. She glanced over once, her hands never stopping on her own patient. Blood pressure dropping. Ultrasound probe revealed fluid in Morrison's pouch. A bleed.

"Prep for emergent laparotomy. Let's go. Don't wait on imaging."

Lucas was already sliding the tube into place. "Visualized the cords. Advancing... bag her. Confirm with CO_2."

"Confirmed," the respiratory tech said, voice taut with relief.

A third patient rolled in—middle-aged woman, alert but clammy. Dr. Shawn Peters stepped in just as the team started triage.

"Need backup?" he asked, already tugging on gloves.

"Bay Two. She's yours," Emily said without looking up. "Monitor, vitals, trauma panel."

Shawn nodded and disappeared into the action.

Minutes blurred.

Emily's patient was wheeled off to the OR, stabilized for now. Lucas's girl was sedated and breathing on her own. Even Shawn gave a quick thumbs-up as his patient's BP normalized.

The room exhaled as the chaos receded, leaving adrenaline and fatigue in its wake.

Emily stood at the sink, washing blood off her hands. She looked over.

Lucas stood by the gurney, jaw tight, expression unreadable.

Their eyes met.

Not a word passed between them.

"That was damn near poetry," Shawn said behind her, cracking open a bottle of water. "You two? Surgical jazz."

Emily didn't respond.

And then the monitors behind them screamed.

Code blue. Bay One.

Emily turned. "That's my boy."

She and Lucas sprinted.

The teen she'd just stabilized was coding—flatline on the screen.

"Where's the cart?" she shouted.

"Here!" Patty pushed it in at full speed.

Lucas moved first. "Starting compressions."

Emily checked the pulse. "Nothing. Push one of epi. Start bagging."

The air closed in. Hands moved. Tools clattered. Lucas's body pressed beside hers, every movement coordinated. As if they'd done this a hundred times before.

It shouldn't have worked—this rhythm, this trust. But with Lucas, it felt like instinct. Like breathing.

He handed her the paddles.

"Clear!"

The boy's chest jerked.

Then—a blip. Another.

A weak, thready rhythm.

Emily released a breath she hadn't realized she was holding. "We're back. Sinus rhythm."

"BP climbing," the nurse said, astonished.

Lucas stepped back, chest heaving.

Patty grinned. "I don't say this lightly, but that was beautiful."

Lucas didn't answer. He stared at the boy like he wasn't quite sure what had just happened either.

Emily wiped sweat from her brow. "You good?"

He nodded. "Just... didn't want another kid to slip away."

She didn't say Lily's name, but it flickered between them all the same.

The locker room was quiet, echoing with the faint hum of fluorescent lights. Lucas twisted his combination lock and opened the door to a wave of steam-scented air from his damp scrubs.

A single piece of paper lay folded on the top shelf.

No envelope. No name.

Just a clean white square.

He opened it.

"Some mistakes don't stay buried."

His fingers froze.

The words felt colder than the tile under his feet.

He nearly crumpled it, fury blooming behind his eyes—but stopped. Instead, he folded the paper neatly and slid it into the back pocket of his jeans, tucked behind his wallet like something that needed remembering.

He turned slowly, eyes scanning the locker room.

Empty.

Still, he couldn't shake the feeling that someone had just left.

Back in the conference room, Emily sat reviewing patient files, her coffee lukewarm, her nerves nowhere near settled.

Shawn leaned against the counter, sipping from a protein shake.

"You and Hayes," he said casually, "make a hell of a team."

Emily didn't look up. "He's competent."

"Competent? You both just resurrected a kid in front of half the night shift."

She clicked a box on the screen. "It's what we're trained to do."

Shawn gave a half smile. "Just saying—interesting timing. Working that closely with the new trauma cowboy? Word travels fast. Especially with board seats still warm."

That got her attention. She raised an eyebrow. "What are you implying?"

"Nothing," he said, voice smooth. "Just that the board likes heroes. Especially quiet ones. And sometimes visibility makes the difference."

Emily stared at him. "And what about doing the right thing?"

Shawn's smile faltered. "That too."

She closed the chart. "We're all here for the same reason, right?"

Shawn picked up his shake. "Sure. We all want to save lives. We just don't all use the same tools."

He left, leaving the room cooler than before.

Lucas stood at the stairwell near the west wing, watching the rain smear the city skyline like bruises on glass.

The note in his pocket felt heavier than it should.

He took it out, unfolded it again.

Read the words.

Then looked up at the exit sign glowing above the door.

Someone knew.

Someone wanted him off balance.

And the clock was already ticking.

Chapter 4 - Midnights Coffee Break

Rooftop Garden – Midnight – The city breathes below; the past lingers above.

The automatic doors hissed open to the rooftop garden, and with them came the scent of rain-soaked concrete, distant blossoms, and something quieter—solace. Emily Carter stepped into the open air and let her shoulders drop. This was her place. Her unofficial chapel, where mistakes couldn't echo louder than the wind. She came here when the walls of St. Theresa's pressed too tight around her.

The night was thick with cloud cover. Lights from the city smeared the sky in a murky halo, as if even the stars were too tired to shine. Water clung to the railing, sparkling like sweat on a pulse.

Emily walked to the far end, near the bench with the broken slat, and leaned into the cool metal rail. Her scrub jacket barely held off the chill, but she didn't care. She reached into her pocket and pulled out an apple. Crisp, red, familiar. The only predictable thing in her life. She turned it over in her hand, not ready to bite.

Behind her, the door whispered open again.

"I had a feeling I'd find you up here," came Lucas Hayes's voice, low and casual—but respectful.

She didn't turn. "You stalking me now?"

"Just developing a healthy appreciation for your escape routes."

He moved in slow, deliberate steps, eventually stopping at the other side of the railing. Not too close. Just within range of shared silence.

"You always work this late?" he asked after a moment.

"Trauma doesn't punch out."

"Neither do ghosts."

She arched a brow at that and finally turned.

Lucas stood with his signature thermos, steam curling lazily from the spout. Even in half-shadow, he looked like he belonged to the city—tired, weathered, stubborn.

"That your homemade concoction?" she asked.

"The one and only. Hazelnut base, oat milk, cinnamon, cardamom, and an espresso shot for good measure."

She blinked. "That's not coffee. That's something served in a goblet at a wizard convention."

Lucas grinned. "Chaos tastes good after midnight."

He poured a bit into the detachable lid and offered it to her. She eyed it like it might bite.

He didn't move. Just waited.

She finally took it and sipped. The warmth hit her tongue with a syrupy kick. Sweet, nutty, almost absurd. But behind it was strength.

"It tastes like insomnia... with sprinkles."

"I'm choosing to be flattered."

They stood together for a beat, the wind threading between them like a third presence.

Emily bit into her apple.

"You always eat those during shift changes," Lucas said.

"They help me focus."

"Or it's superstition."

"And your sugar-bombed caffeine ritual isn't?"

He smirked but said nothing.

Silence stretched again—but it was a gentler one now.

"You ever wonder," he said eventually, "if we chose this life because we needed a place where being broken just meant being useful?"

Emily blinked. "That's... heavier than I expected from someone who smells like gingerbread."

Lucas glanced down. "You're not wrong."

He shifted, leaning on the rail, and for the first time since they'd met, something in his posture softened.

"I screwed up," he said. "At Greystone."

Emily's spine tensed.

Lucas's voice stayed low. "Pediatric trauma case. Boy, six years old. Massive internal bleed. I called for backup. No one came fast enough. So I moved on my own. Stabilized him—barely."

Her grip tightened on the apple.

"He lived," Lucas continued. "But there were complications. Parents were furious. Admin blamed me for going off-protocol. I left before they could make it official."

Emily turned to him slowly. "You didn't walk away. You ran before they could bury you."

Lucas looked at her, and something flickered in his eyes. "Yeah."

She exhaled. She should've felt wary. But instead, she felt a strange pull—a shared gravity between survivors.

"I lost a patient," she said. "Her name was Lily. She was six too."

Lucas didn't move.

"Severe allergic reaction. Seizure hit hard. I hesitated—just long enough to lose her. I see her sometimes, when I scrub in. As if I'm supposed to answer for it every day."

Lucas's voice was soft. "That's why you don't let anyone close."

Emily's throat tightened. "And why you don't ask for help."

They stood in that fragile understanding. The wind hummed around them, carrying off things unspoken.

Lucas reached into his thermos and poured more into the cup. Without comment, he handed it to her again.

She accepted it, then broke off the remaining half of her apple and held it out.

He took it—his fingers brushing hers. Warm. Brief. But it sparked something uncomfortably electric.

Their eyes met. Neither of them moved.

"I think I just witnessed a truce," he said.

"Don't make it weird," she replied, too quietly.

He took a bite. "Tart. Unexpected."

"You'll get used to it."

A soft laugh escaped him. Not the loud, charming kind—but something real.

She sipped the coffee. It was stronger this time. She didn't mind.

"I used to think medicine was about mastery," she said. "But lately, I wonder if it's just endurance."

Lucas nodded. "Or forgiveness. If we're lucky."

They stood in silence, hands occupied, hearts a little less so.

Then the rooftop speakers clicked to life.

"Code blue. Pediatrics. Code blue."

Emily's body went cold. Her mouth moved before she thought.

"Please not another Lily."

Lucas was already moving.

So was she.

They reached the rooftop door together. But before Lucas pulled it open, he paused.

"Emily."

She turned to him.

His voice was quiet. "Do you believe in second chances?"

Her chest tightened. She didn't know if it was from the question or the way he said her name.

"I don't know," she admitted.

Then the door banged open, and they were gone—down the stairwell, toward another emergency, another battlefield of flashing monitors and cracking bones.

But behind them, the question lingered—fragile, flickering, and far from answered.

Chapter 5 - Suspicions and Support

The cafeteria buzzed with its usual blend of overworked staff and undercaffeinated ambition. Trays clattered, heels tapped, and coffee machines hissed like background static. Sunlight filtered through the smudged windows in weak streaks, catching on the rim of Dr. Emily Carter's untouched cup.

She sat at a corner table, shoulders hunched slightly, gaze fixed on the swirling steam rising from her drink. Her hair was damp from the early-morning shower she'd squeezed in after the overnight code blue. Lily's name still pulsed somewhere behind her ribs like a second heartbeat.

Across from her, Nurse Patty Moreno plunked down with an overstuffed egg sandwich and two mini creamers she probably had no intention of using.

"You look like you slept in a linen closet," Patty said, unwrapping her sandwich.

"I didn't sleep."

Patty tore off a bite. "Because of the code blue or the rooftop heart-to-heart with Dr. Complicated?"

Emily arched a brow. "You really do have cameras hidden all over this place."

"I'm the night shift. We *are* the cameras."

Emily offered the faintest smile but didn't reply.

Patty leaned in slightly, softening her tone. "You okay?"

"I don't know." Emily stirred her coffee. "It's easier when I can pretend the past is just static. But last night... it wasn't."

"Because of him?"

"Because of *everything*," she replied, voice barely above a whisper.

Patty nodded. "So, let's talk it out before you combust from repression."

Emily hesitated, then quietly said, "He asked me if I believed in second chances."

"And?"

"I told him I didn't know."

Patty's gaze softened. "That's an honest answer."

"But is it the right one?"

Before Patty could reply, a group of nurses at the next table erupted into whispers.

"I'm telling you," one said, her voice just low enough to sound secretive but just loud enough to be heard. "Lucas Hayes isn't clean. There's a reason no hospital wanted to touch him after Greystone."

Another chimed in. "I heard he doctored a chart to cover up a mistake. The admin at Greystone squashed it to avoid lawsuits."

Patty looked over. "Why don't you say that a little louder so you can be sued in stereo?"

But they ignored her.

A third voice joined in—cool, controlled, and unmistakably deliberate. "There's no need for hostility," said Lindsay Wilcox, the hospital administrator who managed to turn professionalism into a blade. "We just have to be aware. Especially those of us with leadership aspirations."

Emily's back stiffened.

Patty muttered, "Here we go."

Lindsay approached their table with the slow, deliberate gait of someone who believed heels made her important.

She wore her usual immaculate suit and air of superiority like armor.

"Dr. Carter," Lindsay said smoothly. "Lovely to see you. I assume you're aware of the growing concerns about Dr. Hayes's... history."

"I'm aware of gossip," Emily replied.

Lindsay tilted her head. "Gossip often carries a kernel of truth. I would hope, given your aspirations, that you're prioritizing discernment over sentiment."

Patty snorted. "You mean loyalty over slander?"

Lindsay ignored her. "The board is paying close attention to all department leaders right now. And to those aligned with them."

Emily stood, slowly, coffee cup in hand. "If you're suggesting that who I work with disqualifies me from a job, then say it outright. Don't veil it in performance reviews you haven't read yet."

Lindsay smiled, perfectly unbothered. "Some reputations are self-cleaning. Others need a little... polish."

She turned and walked away, heels clicking like punctuation marks.

Patty leaned back. "You want me to 'accidentally' spill soup on her tomorrow? Chicken noodle can do damage."

Emily wanted to laugh. Instead, the unease clung to her ribs like dried blood.

Later that morning, Jasmine Rao intercepted Emily outside the staff elevator.

"Walk with me," she said.

They strolled down the administrative hallway, floor gleaming beneath their feet.

Jasmine didn't speak at first. Emily waited.

"You're being watched," Jasmine said finally. "Not just by the board. By everyone."

"I figured."

"I need you to understand something, Emily," Jasmine continued, tone steady. "Leadership isn't about being perfect. It's about enduring the illusion that you have to be."

Emily glanced at her. "That's not exactly comforting."

"It's not meant to be. It's meant to prepare you."

They reached Jasmine's office. She didn't go inside. Instead, she turned.

"Every leader inherits whispers. What matters is how you move through them. Quietly, clearly, and without apology."

Emily nodded. "And what about allies who come with baggage?"

Jasmine held her gaze. "Then you carry it wisely, or you let it go. But you don't drag it through the hallways."

The conversation ended without ceremony. Emily turned away, unsure if she felt steadier or more unmoored.

An hour later, she returned to the resident locker area to grab a chart she'd left behind. A single piece of paper was taped to her mailbox. No name. No signature. Just one printed sheet.

"Leadership requires distance. You can't lead from beside someone drowning."

Below the quote was a bulleted list:

- Displays emotional partiality

- Questionable clinical alliances

- Overinvolved in high-risk cases

- Lacks appropriate detachment

- **Judgment possibly compromised by proximity to Dr. Hayes**

Emily stared at it, breath catching in her throat. The critiques weren't just generic—they mirrored things she'd heard from her own inner critic. Things she feared others might think but hoped weren't true.

She peeled the paper off the mailbox and folded it sharply in half.

Behind her, the locker room door creaked.

She turned.

No one.

Emily climbed the east stairwell two flights before sitting on the landing. The stairwell was quiet, the kind of quiet only hospitals knew—laced with the hum of life-sustaining machines on other floors, footsteps like ghosts overhead.

She leaned forward, elbows on her knees, and let her head fall into her hands.

Maybe they're right.

Maybe getting close to Lucas—understanding him, defending him—was clouding her vision.

Maybe Lily had taught her to care too much, and now she couldn't unlearn it.

She wanted the Trauma Unit Head role more than anything. Not just for the title—but because it would mean she hadn't failed. Not permanently.

But if the cost was distancing herself from the only person who understood what it meant to live every day carrying loss like a second stethoscope...

She didn't know if she could do it.

She looked up slowly.

Across from her, the paint on the wall was chipped, revealing a scrawl half-covered by years of attempted scrubbing. It read in faded Sharpie: *Trust no one.*

For the first time, it didn't feel paranoid. It felt... familiar.

The hallway outside the stairwell was quieter than usual when she returned. Emily turned the corner and nearly ran into Lindsay Wilcox.

The administrator smiled too quickly.

"Rough morning?" Lindsay asked.

Emily said nothing.

Lindsay tapped the side of her tablet. "You know, this hospital has high standards. It's what makes it excellent. It's also what makes it... selective."

Emily blinked. "Is this more veiled advice?"

"No," Lindsay said plainly. "It's a warning."

Emily met her gaze.

"In this place, spotless records earn promotions. Messy ones earn reminders of where they belong." She paused, her tone silky. "Some people forget that. You might want to remember."

Then she walked away, heels clicking again—faster this time.

Emily watched her go, stomach tight.

Lindsay knew about the anonymous note. Maybe she wrote it.

Or maybe someone else did—and Lindsay just decided to use it.

Either way, Emily was no longer wondering if someone was trying to sabotage her and Lucas.

She knew it.

And someone had already drawn blood.

The only question now was how deep the cut would go.

Chapter 6 – Collateral Affections

The bell above the café door jingled as Emily stepped into the warm, cinnamon-scented cocoon of Brew Theory. It was a quiet haven tucked between two brownstones, with mismatched chairs, faded armchairs, and indie music humming under the hum of espresso machines. The rain pattered against the tall windows, and the barista waved at her like she was a regular. She wasn't—but Michael was.

She spotted her brother instantly. Curled up on a teal armchair with a sketchpad open on one knee and two drinks on the table, Michael Carter looked more like a poet than a dropout med student turned barista philosopher.

His beanie was crooked, his sweater oversized, and his grin unmistakable.

"You look like someone who hasn't slept in a decade," he greeted, standing to hand her one of the mugs.

"Thanks for the honesty," Emily replied dryly, accepting the drink. Her shoulders sagged as she sank into the armchair opposite him. "Also, not inaccurate."

Michael studied her. "Hospital chaos? Or emotional chaos?"

"A combo platter," she said, wrapping both hands around the cup like it might ground her.

They chatted quietly for a few minutes. Emily filled him in on Lucas's dramatic entrance, the fundraiser tension, and the growing rumors. Michael listened, nodding, only interrupting to add sarcastic quips or thoughtful hums.

"You know," he finally said, tapping his cup, "people who try not to feel anything are usually the ones who've felt the most."

Emily smiled faintly. "You mean me?"

"I mean both of you," he said, just as the bell chimed again.

Lucas.

The doctor stood framed in the doorway, rain in his hair and a wary look in his eyes. He scanned the café like a soldier walking into enemy terrain. His smile flickered, never quite reaching his eyes. He spotted them and paused, halfway to turning around.

Michael stood up and waved.

"Dr. Hayes! We've been expecting you."

Lucas hesitated. Then, with a small shrug, he made his way over.

"Hey," he said to Emily, eyes searching hers.

"Hey," she echoed.

Michael gestured to the only remaining seat at their table. "Sit. Pretend you're off-duty. I promise we won't page you."

Lucas chuckled. "I'll take the risk."

He sat down slowly, the tension easing from his shoulders by inches.

"I wasn't crashing your moment," he said after a pause.

"We don't own the place," Emily replied. "You just walked into an ambush of sibling bonding."

"She's the rational one. I'm the emotionally intuitive disappointment," Michael added cheerfully.

Lucas's grin widened. "Sounds familiar."

For the next fifteen minutes, conversation flowed surprisingly smoothly. Michael talked about the hospital's weird vending machine placement and his conspiracy theory that the cafeteria chili had healing properties. Emily laughed more than she expected to. Lucas even loosened up enough to tell a story about his first solo procedure and how he almost fainted.

"A trauma surgeon fainting?" Michael asked, incredulous.

Lucas shrugged. "They had to slap me. It was humbling."

"Bet you don't include that in your resume," Emily said, sipping her drink.

"Only in the footnotes," he murmured.

A comfortable silence settled over them, rare and welcome.

Then, Lucas turned to Emily. "You're not what I expected."

She looked at him. "Disappointed?"

He paused. "Not even close."

Michael raised an eyebrow and leaned back with exaggerated subtlety. "You two are like human bumper cars. Circling close, never quite colliding."

Emily rolled her eyes, but her cheeks warmed. Lucas rubbed the back of his neck, eyes darting toward the window.

"What did you expect, really?" she asked, soft but pointed.

He hesitated. "Someone colder. More calculated. The kind who'd claw her way to the top and never look back."

Emily's brow lifted. "Charming."

"I was wrong," he said. "You care too much, actually. Even when you pretend not to."

Michael cleared his throat theatrically. "Okay, I'm officially the third wheel now."

Emily tossed a napkin at him, but the flush in her cheeks deepened.

Her phone buzzed.

She glanced at the screen and stiffened. Urgent trauma case. Her expression shifted.

Lucas noticed. "Back to the battlefield?"

"Looks like it."

They both stood.

Michael rose too, collecting his sketchpad. "Try not to save everyone before lunch."

Lucas's hand brushed against Emily's as they reached for their coats. Just a second—warm, unplanned, skin meeting skin.

She froze. So did he.

Then he pulled back. As he adjusted his stethoscope, Emily noticed something: his hand trembled slightly.

A thousand questions rose in her throat, but she swallowed them all. The café had gone quiet, or maybe it was just her pulse thudding in her ears.

Michael leaned toward her. "You're both hiding behind trauma like it's armor. Eventually, you either take it off or collapse beneath it."

Emily exhaled shakily. "You should really charge for that kind of wisdom."

"First one's free. After that, it costs a latte and a pastry."

They stepped into the rain together, umbrellas forgotten. Drops slicked Emily's curls and glistened on Lucas's lashes. They walked in silence down the block, close enough their arms brushed.

And even though no promises had been made, something had shifted. Something warm and tentative, standing its ground against the cold drizzle.

Chapter 7 – Emergency Surgery Collaboration

The call came in at 3:17 a.m.

Emily was half-asleep on the staff lounge sofa, her head propped on a rolled-up hoodie, a medical journal sliding off her lap. The buzz of her pager jolted her upright, heart racing before her brain had even caught up. A trauma code. High-priority. Prepping for surgery.

She blinked away sleep and bolted upright. The corridors of St. Theresa's were eerily quiet at this hour, lights dimmed to a soft glow that made the hospital feel like a cathedral of whispered prayers and anxious footsteps.

Lucas was already at the scrub station when she arrived at OR 3. His surgical cap was slightly crooked, his eyes shadowed from lack of sleep but alert. He focused on the sterile rhythm of his scrub, but his mind betrayed him—flashing back to a surgical theater bathed in accusation and disbelief. Not today. Not here. He could still hear the whispers from his old OR, the ones that turned admiration into suspicion. Tonight had to be different.

"Thought you might beat me here," he said, glancing over. His voice was rough, but not unkind.

Emily didn't smile. She was too keyed up.

"Blunt abdominal trauma," she said. "Motorcycle crash. Helmeted, but the liver's torn and the spleen might be worse. GCS eight. They're rolling him in now."

Lucas nodded once. "Let's move."

Inside the operating room, the air shifted. The heat, the sterility, the adrenaline—it all converged into a hum that Emily felt in her bones. The patient was wheeled in, blood pressure crashing, the trauma team barking vitals, passing clamps, suctioning.

Emily scrubbed in and moved to assist without hesitation, falling into rhythm with Lucas as if their bodies had memorized each other's instincts. His hand reached for the scalpel. Hers was already handing it to him.

"Midline incision," he said, calm but clipped.

"Retractors ready," she replied, voice matching his cadence.

The tension was thick. But in that room—under the blinding surgical lights, surrounded by sterile metal and bloodied gauze—they moved as one. Emily suctioned as Lucas dissected. He clamped a bleeder, she packed the cavity. Their communication was silent more often than spoken. Their eyes met across the operating table—a flicker of understanding passed between them, sharper than any scalpel.

At one point, a nurse dropped a clamp. The metallic clatter jolted everyone.

Lucas didn't even flinch. "Another. Now."

"Vitals dipping," the anesthesiologist warned.

Emily's heart stuttered. "Hang more units. Get me a second line."

Lucas's brow furrowed. "We're missing something. Bleeding—too fast."

She scanned the field. "Left renal artery. Torn. It's behind the hematoma. We need exposure."

Lucas nodded. "I'm going for it. Suction here. Hold steady."

The moment stretched.

He maneuvered deftly, every motion precise. The bleeder came into view, pulsing like a warning. He clamped, tied off. The room exhaled.

The monitor beeped steady.

"Nice catch," Lucas murmured.

Emily didn't look up. "You didn't blink."

"Neither did you."

As silence settled over the bay and monitors steadied, Lucas reached for a towel. Emily's hands brushed his—no chaos now, only breathless stillness. Their hands lingered longer than necessary in the shared silence, the hum of the hospital fading around them. Something electric passed between them, not born of adrenaline—but possibility.

By the time they were closing, the worst had passed. Nurses whispered in awe. The patient's vitals had stabilized, the bleeding controlled. What began as a probable loss had turned into a tentative win.

Lucas peeled off his gloves, tossing them into the bin with a heavy sigh. Sweat darkened the collar of his scrubs.

"You were solid in there," he said, voice low.

Emily stripped off her gown. "So were you."

Outside the OR, silence waited to swallow them again. The hospital always seemed to hold its breath after a save like this.

Lucas leaned against the wall, closing his eyes briefly. "I miss this. The clarity."

Emily nodded. "No politics. Just medicine."

He looked at her. Really looked.

"We make a good team."

It hung there, suspended. Not just about surgery.

Emily swallowed. Her chest felt too tight. "We do."

Before she could say more, Jasmine appeared at the end of the corridor.

She approached with measured steps, eyes flitting between them.

Jasmine watched silently, her sharp eyes missing nothing. When her gaze lingered a second longer on Emily, it wasn't just professional curiosity—it was calculation.

"That was exceptional work," she said. "The board will be informed. But in this hospital, excellence attracts scrutiny. Be careful where your strengths are seen."

Emily straightened. "Thank you, Dr. Rao."

Lucas's jaw tightened, but he didn't speak. Jasmine nodded once more and walked off.

The corridor stretched silent again.

Emily sighed. "That was a compliment and a warning."

Lucas smirked, but it didn't reach his eyes. "Welcome to St. Theresa's."

They stood there for a long moment. Tired. Wired. Unwilling to leave the space they had carved for themselves—even if it was only in that OR, only for a while.

Then a code was called overhead, and they parted without another word.

But something had changed.

In blood and urgency, under pressure and light, something new had taken root.

Chapter 8 – Shadows in the Hall

T he morning came too soon.

Emily leaned over the nurses' station, exhaustion in every muscle, a steaming coffee in her hand and the acrid tang of antiseptic in her nose. Her scrubs clung to her back, damp from adrenaline and exertion. She hadn't slept since the emergency surgery with Lucas. Not that she would have been able to.

The feel of his hand brushing hers during cleanup. The steady beat of his voice across the sterile field. The unspoken connection. It had shaken her.

She hadn't told anyone. Not even Patty.

"You look like you've gone twelve rounds with a trauma bay," said Shawn Peters, sliding a folder onto the desk beside her. His grin was too polished for someone who'd just started his shift.

"I did," Emily replied dryly, flipping through a patient chart. "You're welcome."

Shawn chuckled, but his eyes narrowed slightly as he studied her face. "You and Lucas worked that case together, right? Heard the save was damn near surgical poetry."

Emily didn't look up. "We did our jobs."

He leaned closer. "That all you did?"

Before she could answer, Patty appeared, carrying a clipboard and two protein bars. She handed one to Emily with a raised brow.

"Play nice, Shawn," Patty said sweetly. "Some of us are running on cortisol and sarcasm."

Shawn held up his hands in mock surrender. "Hey, I just admire good teamwork."

Patty gave him a pointed look before turning to Emily. "You okay? You haven't blinked since I got here."

Emily forced a smile. "I'm fine. Just running through post-op notes."

But the moment they were alone, Patty leaned in. "Are you going to tell me what really happened last night, or do I have to bribe the OR nurse?"

Emily sighed, rubbing her temples. "Nothing happened. We handled the trauma, and it went well. That's all."

Patty narrowed her eyes. "Right. And the moon is made of gauze."

Before Emily could retort, Jasmine Rao appeared at the end of the corridor. Her tailored lab coat flowed behind her like a cape, and her expression was unreadable. She approached with quiet authority.

"Dr. Carter," she said. "A moment?"

Emily exchanged a look with Patty, then followed Jasmine into a private consultation room. The door closed behind them with a click.

"I spoke with the board this morning," Jasmine began, folding her arms. "They've received another anonymous complaint regarding Dr. Hayes."

Emily's heart sank. "About what, specifically?"

"Impropriety. Blurred lines between professional and personal conduct."

Emily opened her mouth to defend him but stopped short.

"They're watching, Emily," Jasmine continued, her voice low. "And not just Lucas. You're in contention for the Trauma Unit lead. That spotlight burns hotter than you think."

Emily swallowed hard. "We didn't do anything wrong."

"That won't stop them from believing you did."

Emily's stomach clenched. It wasn't just about career ambition anymore—it was about trust, about truth. And for the first time, she felt the weight of someone else's battles pressing into her own.

Silence settled between them.

"For what it's worth," Jasmine added, "I believe in both of you. But tread carefully."

Emily nodded and exited the room, pulse pounding. She needed air.

She cut through the administrative wing, where long halls echoed with the click of heels and hushed conversations. The walls felt too close, the overhead lights too harsh. She paused outside the records office, where the scent of old files and copy toner spilled into the hallway.

Inside, Lindsay Wilcox stood over a file cabinet, sharply dressed and smugly composed. Emily felt her stomach twist.

"Well, if it isn't St. Theresa's golden girl," Lindsay said without turning. "How's our trauma hero this morning?"

Emily folded her arms. "Just passing through."

Lindsay shut the drawer with a decisive clack. "I hear your friend Dr. Hayes is attracting quite the audience."

"If you have something to say, Lindsay, say it."

Lindsay turned, eyes glinting. "Reputation is everything here. Doesn't take much to crack a polished surface. Especially when that surface is already under a microscope."

Emily stepped closer. "Careful, Lindsay. The more you stir the pot, the easier it is to get burned."

"I don't need to spread anything," Lindsay said smoothly. "People talk. And they listen."

She brushed past Emily and walked off, heels echoing like a metronome of menace.

Emily exhaled sharply. Lindsay was behind this—she was sure of it. But proving it? That was another matter.

Later that afternoon, Emily found Lucas in the staff lounge, alone with a sandwich large enough to require structural reinforcement. He looked up, surprised but not displeased.

"You want half?"

She sat beside him. "Only if it comes with intel."

He raised a brow. "What kind of intel?"

"Someone's trying to sink you. Again."

Lucas set down his sandwich. "Let me guess. Wilcox."

Emily nodded. "She's whispering to the board. Anonymous complaints. Same playbook."

Lucas looked away. "I knew it would follow me here."

Emily studied him. "You could fight it."

He shook his head. "Last time I tried that, they accused me of defensiveness. This time, I figured I'd just keep my head down."

"That only works if they let you."

Lucas laughed, but it was hollow. "You don't need this mess, Emily. You're aiming for something bigger. Don't let me drag you down."

Emily surprised herself. "Maybe I don't want to climb if it means stepping over people I care about."

Lucas looked at her then, really looked. His expression softened, wounded pride warring with a flicker of something unguarded.

"You care?"

She hesitated, then nodded. "Yeah. I think I do."

Lucas's fingers brushed hers on the table. Just once. But the contact lingered in the air long after it was gone.

The door opened suddenly. Patty slipped in, blinking at the heavy silence. "Interrupting something?"

Emily stood. "No. We were just... strategizing."

Patty gave Lucas a once-over and smirked. "Hope your strategy includes taking down hospital dragons."

Emily left the lounge with a new fire in her step. She couldn't protect Lucas with wishes—but maybe she could with facts.

She headed toward the security office.

Because if there was one thing hospitals did better than saving lives, it was watching them. Somewhere in the surveillance archives—perhaps a time-stamped recording, a misaligned accusation—lay the truth. Or the final nail in Lucas's coffin.

Cliffhanger: Emily discovers archived surveillance footage that may prove Lucas was innocent—or not.

Chapter 9 – Eyes Behind Glass

The security office at St. Theresa's was tucked behind the loading dock, a boxy room filled with monitors, blinking lights, and the quiet hum of servers. Emily knocked lightly before stepping inside. The overhead fluorescents buzzed like agitated bees.

"Help you, Doctor?" asked the man behind the desk, his nameplate reading R. Cabot. He looked like he'd rather be anywhere else.

Emily offered a polite smile, though her stomach was tight with nerves. "I'm looking for surveillance footage from two nights ago. ICU corridor, post-op wing. I need to review something. It's important."

Cabot squinted at her over the rim of his glasses. "You got clearance?"

"Chief Rao knows I'm here. I can have her confirm it."

He sighed, typing slowly into the system. After a long pause, he gestured to a seat beside him. "Ten-minute limit. I ain't running a cinema."

Emily sat down, the chair creaking beneath her. The screen flickered with grainy footage from hallway cameras. She scrubbed through hours of timestamped silence, fast-forwarding past nurses, gurneys, and janitorial carts.

Then she saw it.

Emily's breath caught. She leaned in closer, heart thudding against her ribs like a warning drum. It wasn't just the contact—it was the way Lucas froze, like prey sensing a trap.

Lucas. Standing alone outside the ICU door.

He looked tense, glancing around. Then Lindsay entered the frame. They spoke. She stepped close—too close. Her hand grazed his arm, and though Lucas didn't recoil, he stiffened. His jaw tensed, eyes flicking away like he wanted to be anywhere else.

Seconds later, she turned abruptly and walked away, tossing something into the nearby trash.

Emily paused the footage. Her heart pounded.

Cabot leaned over. "That what you were looking for?"

"Can you isolate that clip and send it to Chief Rao? And to me?"

"Sure."

As he typed, Emily stood and approached the trash bin from the video—still in the same hallway. Nothing was in it now. But she jotted the bin's ID and date anyway.

She had something. Not proof, but a thread.

Back in the main hospital, Emily walked the long corridor with her thoughts storming. Her shoes echoed against the floor tiles, heart hammering louder with each step. She passed familiar faces—Patty laughing with a transport tech, Jasmine moving briskly between meetings, interns hunched over clipboards—but they blurred around her.

She found Jasmine in her office, phone pressed to her ear.

"No, Board Member Crane, I do not believe disciplinary action is appropriate without evidence," Jasmine was saying.

Emily paused at the door until Jasmine ended the call.

"Let me guess," Jasmine said, rubbing her temple. "You have something."

Emily nodded. "Footage. Lindsay approached Lucas. Made contact. Then she threw something away. Timing aligns with the complaint."

Jasmine exhaled, a hint of relief crossing her face. "Forward it to me. I'll escalate it."

"They're still pushing, aren't they?"

"Harder than ever. Board Member Crane in particular. He wants Lucas suspended."

Emily frowned. "Why?"

Jasmine hesitated. "Let's just say Crane has his own vision for who should lead this hospital. And Lucas isn't part of it."

Emily nodded slowly. "Then we better make sure he can't rig the outcome." Her voice was low, firm. She wasn't just defending a colleague—she was drawing a line, one she had no intention of erasing. Her voice was low, firm. She wasn't just defending a colleague—she was drawing a line.

Later that evening, Lucas was charting notes in an empty exam room when Emily found him. The room was dimly lit, only the glow from a tablet screen illuminating his face.

"You're being targeted," she said bluntly.

He glanced up, eyes tired. "I figured."

"I found footage. It helps. I sent it to Jasmine."

He set down his pen. "Why are you doing this, Emily? You don't owe me anything."

She stepped further into the room, closing the door behind her. "Maybe I do. Or maybe I'm just tired of watching good doctors get destroyed by politics."

He stood, expression unreadable. "You keep risking things for me. It's not just professional, is it?"

Emily didn't look away. "No. It's not."

She remembered the first time she saw Lucas under surgical lights—calm, precise, unshakable. Now, shadows lingered in his eyes. She hated seeing him like this.

A silence settled, not awkward but thick with unspoken things.

Lucas reached into his coat pocket and pulled out a folded piece of paper. He handed it to her.

It was a printout of an anonymous message: "Step back or you'll fall too."

"Someone left it in my locker this morning," he said quietly.

Emily's eyes narrowed. A chill crept over her skin. She glanced toward the door, suddenly aware of how alone they were. "Then we're closer than I thought. They're scared."

He gave a humorless laugh. "That's one way to look at it."

Emily folded the note again, her hands steady despite the pounding in her chest. "I'll take this to Jasmine, too. We'll need to show a pattern."

"You really trust her?"

"With my job? Yes. With my heart? Not yet."

Lucas smiled, the expression small but real. "Thanks. For everything."

She lingered another moment, watching him. "You should get some sleep. You look like hell."

"Thanks, Dr. Carter. Always a charmer."

She smiled and turned to leave.

But as she stepped into the hallway, her hospital inbox buzzed on her phone. Subject line: Look again. You missed it.

The message contained only a file attachment—no name, no note.

Emily's blood ran cold. She hesitated, thumb hovering over the screen. Whatever was in that file, she knew—this wasn't over. It was only just beginning.

Cliffhanger: A new board vote is scheduled. Crane plans to push for Lucas's suspension. But the footage file Emily receives holds something she never expected—someone else entirely near the trash bin... someone who wasn't supposed to be there.

Chapter 10 – The Enemy Within

Emily locked herself in the resident workroom and opened the mysterious file on her phone. The footage was timestamped five minutes after Lindsay walked away from the trash bin. At first, the hallway appeared empty—dim and still. But then a figure stepped into frame.

Not a nurse. Not a doctor.

Board Member Crane.

He walked slowly, looking behind him, then toward the camera. For a brief second, his hand reached into the trash bin—the same bin Lindsay had used. He withdrew something, tucked it inside his jacket, then moved out of frame.

Emily froze, her heart thudding. Her stomach twisted. Crane. Of all people. The man shaking hands in boardrooms was rifling through trash like a thief. This wasn't a misunderstanding or hospital gossip. This was a setup. A coordinated one. And now she was in the middle of it.

She copied the file to her secure folder and forwarded it to Jasmine with a single line: *We need to talk. Immediately.*

A knock on the door startled her.

It was Lucas.

"I just got pulled into a meeting with Crane," he said. "Alone. No witness. He said the board is voting tomorrow morning. If I don't submit a letter of resignation by midnight, he'll call for suspension."

Emily stood up, fury igniting in her chest. "That's blackmail."

Lucas looked tired. Resigned. "He said he's trying to protect the hospital from scandal."

"By threatening a decorated trauma surgeon?"

"By erasing me before questions can be asked."

Emily reached into her pocket and handed him her phone. "Watch this."

Lucas watched the footage in silence. When Crane appeared onscreen, his jaw locked.

"I knew something was off," he said softly. "I didn't think it went this deep."

"Lindsay was the bait. Crane is the one pulling the strings."

Lucas looked at her, emotion flashing in his eyes. "Why are you still helping me? After everything... after how distant I was."

Emily stepped closer. She thought back to those first nights in the ER—his quiet steadiness, the way he'd stayed an hour past shift just to help a dying patient's family. "Because I remember the version of you they're trying to erase. And I won't let them rewrite your story."

He looked down. "If they come after you..."

"Let them try."

They stood there for a moment, breath mingling in the stillness. He reached out, just brushing her hand with his.

Then her phone buzzed again. Jasmine.

Conference room. Now.

Jasmine had already dimmed the lights in the conference room. Emily entered first, Lucas behind her.

Jasmine turned from the screen. "I saw the footage. That's Crane."

Emily nodded. "And he took something from the trash."

Jasmine pinched the bridge of her nose. "Three years ago, Crane and Lindsay worked together on the board of a hospital in Seattle. There was an internal scandal involving tampered incident reports. Whistleblowers disappeared, files vanished. Nothing stuck, but Lindsay left soon after."

Lucas shook his head. "And now they're doing it again. Here."

Jasmine opened a folder on the table. "This came to me anonymously a week ago. I thought it was paranoia. Now I'm not so sure."

Inside was a printout: a formal complaint filed against Crane from a nurse at St. Theresa's. Dated two years prior. The name was redacted, but the complaint was eerily similar to what was happening now. The nurse left the hospital six months later. No forwarding contact.

Emily clenched her fists. "How deep does this go?"

Jasmine looked at both of them. "If we go public, we risk the board turning on all of us. If we stay quiet, Crane gets what he wants."

Lucas crossed his arms. "Then we make noise. I'm not resigning. Let him try to suspend me. But we need proof—more than this."

Emily's eyes narrowed. "I know where to look."

Later that night, Emily returned to the admin wing. The building was mostly empty, lights dimmed. She used Jasmine's borrowed ID to access the restricted HR archive.

Inside, rows of file cabinets lined the walls. She moved quickly, searching the digital index. A file labeled *INTERNAL ETHICS: CLASSIFIED* blinked at her.

She opened it.

Inside were documented complaints. Altered incident reports. Email threads between Crane and Lindsay, filled with carefully coded language. One message read: *Leverage secured. Ensure his removal proceeds by Friday.*

Emily took photos of every page, heart pounding. She paused as she reached a particularly damning image—a scanned copy of an unsigned memo drafted to the board, detailing Lucas's alleged misconduct. The metadata showed it had been created days before the supposed incident with Lindsay.

Her breath caught. They'd planned it.

Another file linked to hospital procurement logs showed Crane had bypassed protocol to secure surveillance access months ago. He'd had eyes on staff long before this scandal began.

A chill ran down her spine.

Then a soft click—too deliberate to be accidental.

The office door creaked open. Cold air rushed in.

She turned, heart in her throat.

A silhouette filled the doorway, just beyond the threshold, face hidden in shadow.

For a heartbeat, no one moved.

Emily didn't breathe. Her grip tightened around her phone. Every survival instinct screamed at her to run.

And then—footsteps retreating. Fast. The echo of hard soles against linoleum faded down the hallway.

She waited three seconds, then bolted to the side exit, heart hammering in her ears.

She had what they needed.

But someone knew she was coming.

And now, they were watching.

Outside, the night air was sharp and damp. Fog drifted low across the lot. Emily slid into her car, locked the doors, and started the engine. Her fingers trembled as she tapped out a message to Lucas and Jasmine:

Got it. Meet me at the safe drop. Now.

She looked in the rearview mirror.

A pair of headlights flicked on behind her.

And didn't move.

Chapter 11 – Crossroads

Emily gripped the steering wheel tighter as she exited the parking lot. Her rearview mirror glared with twin headlights that mirrored her every turn. Whoever was behind her wasn't just leaving work late. They were following her.

She took a sudden left down a side street, then cut through a residential neighborhood. The car followed. Not aggressively—but deliberately.

Her mind raced. Was this someone from Crane's camp? A hospital security tail? Or something worse? Her pulse thudded in her ears, each second amplifying the tension tightening in her chest.

She turned again, this time onto a dark side road leading to an abandoned parking lot behind the old maintenance building. As she slowed and flipped off her headlights, the trailing car passed by without stopping. Emily stayed still, barely breathing, until the taillights disappeared into the distance.

Only then did she exhale, the pounding in her chest slowly easing.

Only then did she exhale.

Her phone buzzed with a new message from Lucas:

On my way. You okay?

She typed back quickly: *Yes. Someone was following. Lost them. Meet at drop point.*

The drop point was a small security locker in the staff gym basement—a place Jasmine had once used to pass sensitive documents. She parked at the far end of the lot and stepped out, her sneakers echoing faintly across the concrete. Fog clung low to the pavement, softening the world into shadows and silence.

She reached the locker, slid the documents inside, and locked it. Her hands were shaking.

Moments later, Lucas and Jasmine arrived in separate cars. Lucas exited his vehicle first, his eyes sweeping the area before he moved to her side.

"You sure you lost them?" he asked.

"I'm sure. But they were close. Too close."

Jasmine nodded. "We have to assume they know we're on to them. That makes this next step even riskier."

Emily handed her the locker key. "The documents are in there. Enough to expose Crane, and maybe bring down Lindsay with him."

Jasmine looked at it like it was a lit fuse, as if it might explode in her hands. Her throat tightened. She'd fought too hard to get where she was—burning it down would mean risking everything. But she also knew what was right. That war inside her showed in the slight tremble of her fingers. "We leak this, we burn every bridge we've got. There's no going back."

Lucas glanced between them. "Then we go forward. All the way."

The next morning, the hospital buzzed with tension. Rumors rippled through departments like tremors before a quake. Everyone knew something was happening. No one knew what.

Emily dressed in dark slacks and a crisp blazer, tying her hair back. As she entered the staff lounge, conversations hushed. Some people nodded respectfully. Others avoided her gaze. She didn't care.

She found Lucas already waiting, arms crossed, jaw tight. His phone chimed with a text. He read it and passed it to Emily.

Board meeting at 9. Crane wants you there.

Emily read it twice. "They're going to try to corner you."

Lucas nodded. "Then let them try."

They walked together to the executive floor. Jasmine met them outside the boardroom, already mid-call.

"We have reporters on standby," she said as she hung up. "Three outlets. If this meeting goes sideways, the leak drops."

Emily blinked, surprise flickering across her face. Jasmine had always been strategic, but this was bold—even reckless. "You told the press?"

Jasmine didn't flinch. "I told the truth. It's time they heard it."

Inside, the boardroom was polished, cold. Crane sat at the head of the long table, flanked by Lindsay and three other senior members. Their faces were masks of concern and judgment.

"Dr. Hayes," Crane began. "Thank you for coming. This won't take long."

Lucas didn't sit. Neither did Emily.

Crane cleared his throat. "The board has reviewed the conduct allegations. Given the nature of the events and the reputational risk to St. Theresa's, we are prepared to proceed with a motion for temporary suspension unless you tender your resignation."

Jasmine stepped forward and placed a folder on the table.

"Before you do that," she said, "you might want to see this."

Crane opened it slowly. Inside were printed emails, procurement logs, complaint records, and the damning surveillance photo.

His expression shifted.

"Where did you get this?"

"That part doesn't matter," Jasmine replied. "What matters is the truth."

Lucas stared him down. "You tried to frame me. You used Lindsay to bait me, altered evidence, manipulated records. And now it's over."

Crane stood, slow and menacing. "You don't understand the implications of what you're doing."

Emily stepped forward. "No, I do. I'm protecting my colleagues. My patients. This hospital. From people like you."

Crane glanced around the room, searching for support.

One board member cleared his throat. "This... requires review."

Another nodded. "These are serious accusations. If proven..."

Crane's face twisted, then smoothed into practiced calm. "Of course. Due process."

But Emily saw the rage behind his eyes. And something else.

Fear.

An hour later, outside the boardroom, Emily, Lucas, and Jasmine huddled in the corridor.

"It worked," Jasmine said. "Crane's been placed on leave pending investigation. Lindsay's status is under review."

Lucas let out a long breath. Relief washed over his features.

"This isn't over," Emily said. "He won't go quietly."

Jasmine shrugged. "Then we'll be louder."

Lucas looked at Emily. His voice softened. "You didn't have to stand by me. But you did."

She met his gaze, eyes steady. Inside, her chest tightened—not with fear, but something deeper. For all the times she'd doubted him, doubted herself, this moment felt right. "I wanted to."

For the first time in weeks, a tentative smile tugged at his lips.

Outside the hospital, the morning light broke through the thinning fog.

But Emily knew the storm hadn't passed.

It had just changed direction.

And she was ready for whatever came next.

Chapter 12 – Veins of Smoke

The rain had returned. Soft at first, then steady, soaking the pavement outside St. Theresa's and giving the hospital's facade a slick, silver sheen. Emily sat inside the dim staff lounge, her fingers wrapped around a paper cup of lukewarm coffee, eyes fixed on the reflection of water sliding down the window. Her thoughts drifted—not just to the boardroom standoff, but to the creeping sense that peace was a mirage. Every calm moment felt like the breath before a scream. The hospital, her haven once, now felt like a trap she couldn't escape.

Lucas hadn't spoken much since the boardroom battle. She couldn't blame him. He'd been forced to defend not just his career, but his integrity—again. And even with

Crane temporarily out, shadows lingered in every hallway, watching.

"They're still here," Jasmine had warned earlier that morning. "Just quieter. Waiting."

Emily took a sip of coffee, grimacing at the bitterness. The aftertaste reminded her of how unfinished it all felt. She pulled out her tablet and began scanning through the day's incident logs. There had been three reports of unauthorized access attempts to the sub-basement server room in the last two weeks. All dismissed as technical glitches. She didn't believe in that kind of coincidence anymore.

Her phone buzzed. A text.

Code Blue. OR 2.

Emily was on her feet before the caffeine could hit. She dropped the cup and sprinted through the hallway, badge swinging. Doors blurred past in a rush of sterile white and flashing lights. Her shoes squeaked across polished tile. Overhead, the intercom droned with static, then silence.

She reached the operating room just as the trauma team was wheeling in a male patient. Gunshot wound. Mid-thirties. Heavy bleeding. The surgeon on duty barked orders.

"He was found near the hospital entrance," a nurse said to Emily. "Collapsed right outside. No ID."

Lucas entered seconds later, eyes locking with hers.

"What the hell...?" he muttered, then stepped in to assist.

The scene became a blur of suction tubes, clamps, blood, and barked instructions. Emily held pressure while Lucas navigated the shredded artery. The room pulsed with urgency. Monitors beeped in erratic rhythm. A nurse slipped on the wet floor but caught herself.

"He's crashing!" the anesthesiologist shouted.

"BP dropping!"

"Got it—clamp!" Lucas said.

Emily handed him what he needed, her breath coming in short, calculated bursts. She counted silently with the monitor's beeps, anchoring herself in rhythm and focus. Every second mattered.

Finally, the monitor leveled. Stabilized.

Lucas nodded. "He's holding. For now."

Emily stepped back, chest rising and falling. Blood painted the cuffs of her sleeves. The metallic tang lingered in her nose.

They met eyes, but neither spoke.

Inside, Emily felt like she was unraveling—one stitch at a time. Not from the blood, not from the trauma, but from the certainty that this man hadn't arrived by chance.

Later, in the scrub room, Emily peeled off her gloves and scrub top. Her hands trembled, not from exhaustion—from what she'd seen.

A tattoo.

On the man's inner forearm.

A jagged mark. Familiar. Too familiar.

She had seen it before. Not in a clinic, not on a patient—but in the folder Jasmine had uncovered. The symbol had haunted her dreams since—something about it reeked of menace, of something buried deep that now clawed its way to the surface. She remembered the photos in Jasmine's file—marked corpses, gang affiliations, redacted memos. The symbol was always there, lurking in the corners.

She closed her eyes, the memory striking her like a defibrillator shock. It was the same symbol from the folder Jasmine had uncovered—the off-the-books supplier linked to Crane's backdoor dealings. A gang tag, associated with an organized trafficking ring known for laundering funds through shell nonprofits.

She grabbed a towel, pressed it to her face, and tried to slow her thoughts.

A knock at the door.

Lucas entered, his shirt damp from sweat and rain. He leaned against the lockers, watching her.

"You saw it too," she said.

He nodded. "Same symbol."

Emily leaned back. "That can't be a coincidence."

"It's not."

"They brought someone into our hospital—to send a message? Or he was running from them. Either way, he ended up bleeding out on our doorstep."

Lucas's jaw tightened. "He wasn't running from them. He was bringing something."

Emily blinked. "What?"

"They found something in his jacket," Lucas said. He pulled out a folded slip of paper and handed it to her.

With trembling fingers, she unfolded the slip. Just one line stared back at her, clean and mechanical—as if typed by someone who didn't want to leave fingerprints.

Emily Carter.

The letters blurred for a second. Her name—printed, deliberate. Not scrawled in panic or happenstance. She gripped the paper tighter. Was it a warning? A target? Or a cry for help? Her breath hitched as the implication sank in—this wasn't random.

She stared at it.

Her heart pounded.

"This isn't over," Lucas said. "It's getting worse."

Emily didn't answer. The room spun around her.

This wasn't just hospital politics anymore.

It was something darker.

Larger.

And she was at the center of it.

She wasn't just part of the story anymore. She was the next chapter. And someone had already started writing it.

As rain streaked the scrub room window like veins of smoke, Emily stared into the storm, wondering just how deep this would go.

Outside, the ambulance bay echoed with distant sirens. Somewhere in the city, something else was falling apart. Emily's phone buzzed again, but she didn't look. Not yet.

Her name wasn't just on a slip of paper.

It was on someone's list.

And lists like that always came with a price.

Chapter 13 – The Whisper Protocol

R ain splattered across the windows like static, a relentless hiss that filled the stillness of Lucas's on-call room. Emily stood just inside the doorway, her scrubs still damp, her eyes wide and shadowed. Lucas sat hunched at the desk, a secure laptop open, screen casting a cold glow across his face.

"Tell me again what Jasmine found," he said without looking up.

Emily hesitated. "Back-door funding trails. Off-book patient files. One flagged memo about something called 'The Whisper Protocol.'"

Lucas's fingers paused over the keyboard. "It wasn't just a test program."

She stepped closer, the air between them charged. "Then what was it?"

Lucas pulled up a buried directory Jasmine had decrypted. "It was a psychological monitoring initiative. Real-time EEG monitoring of coma patients—supposedly to study trauma recovery. But then it shifted."

"Shifted how?" Emily asked.

"Toward something more invasive," he said. "Dream induction. Memory disruption. They experimented with neural feedback loops. There were reports of patients experiencing night terrors, disassociation… one of them died during phase two."

Emily's throat tightened. "So they buried it."

He nodded. "Scrubbed the archive, shut it down—but not before six patients were listed as 'terminated.'"

Lucas clicked one final time and a name appeared on screen.

Subject 07 – Terminated.

No other details. Just a date. Just a file ID.

Emily crossed her arms to still her trembling. "We need more."

Before he could respond, her hospital inbox pinged.

A new message.

No sender. No subject.

Emily clicked it open.

Stop digging.

No signature. No metadata. The text dissolved seconds after opening.

She stared at the blank screen.

"They're watching us," she whispered.

Lucas stood slowly. "Then we stay ahead of them."

Their eyes met, and something between fear and fury flared in Emily's chest. "Why didn't you tell me this ran so deep?"

"Because I didn't want to drag you into something I still don't understand."

"But I'm already in it." She turned to face him fully. "They dropped a man with my name in his pocket on our OR table."

Lucas's breath caught. "I know."

"And still you keep holding back?"

"I'm trying to protect you, Emily—"

She closed the distance between them in two steps. "Then stop treating me like I'm fragile."

The space between them sparked. The air thickened.

Lucas reached for her, slow but sure, cupping the side of her face like she might vanish. "You think I don't lie awake at night wondering how to keep you from breaking?"

"I already broke," she whispered.

Lucas kissed her.

It wasn't gentle.

It was months of frustration, fear, guilt, and longing colliding all at once.

Emily leaned into him, her hands sliding up beneath his shirt, feeling the warmth of his skin, the muscle coiled beneath. His fingers tangled in her damp hair. She gasped into his mouth, every thought dissolving into heat, urgency, the sense that they were standing on a ledge and finally, finally jumping.

He lifted her to the desk, the laptop clattering aside.

She broke the kiss, chest heaving. "Lucas—"

He froze instantly. "Too much?"

"No," she said, voice raw. "Just... I don't want this to be another thing we hide."

Lucas pressed his forehead to hers. "Then don't. Don't hide with me. Fight."

Their mouths met again—slower this time, reverent—but Emily pulled back before it could spiral.

She slid off the desk, grounding herself. Her heart raced, but her thoughts were louder.

You let yourself feel this. You trusted him. Now trust yourself.

"I have to go," she said quietly.

Lucas didn't argue. He just watched her gather herself, eyes heavy with everything unspoken.

Down in Medical Records, the corridors were silent.

Emily moved with purpose, every step echoing against tile and concrete. She used her clearance badge, then Jasmine's override key to access the secure archive server. Dust motes floated like ghosts as the electronic drawer clicked open.

She typed in the patient ID from earlier.

Accessing file...

Dr. Ryan Mercer – Authorizing Physician.

Her heart dropped.

The document was heavily redacted. Pages of black bars and clinical jargon. But one word kept jumping out:

Experimental.

Then a phrase:

Subject failed to respond to phase two neurochemical induction.

And below it:

Order: Terminated.

Emily's breath hitched. She staggered back from the screen.

Ryan had always been guarded, precise—but never cruel. Never complicit.

But this...

She could still hear his voice from a week ago:

"Some files were above my pay grade back then."

Had he lied? Or had he been covering for something darker?

Her pulse thundered in her ears.

Then a soft sound behind her.

A footstep. Slow. Bare.

She turned sharply.

The door was closing.

No one was there.

Emily stood frozen, her breath locked in her chest. Her name was on a list. Her past was no longer buried. And someone in the hospital still wanted her silent.

Chapter 14 – Blood and Silence

Emily didn't sleep. Her mind churned with jagged fragments—flashes of the archive room, the phantom footstep, the heavy silence pressing in like fog. Her skin crawled as if the night itself were watching her.

She barely made it back to her apartment before dawn, heart still hammering in her chest from the whisper of that footstep, the soft click of the archive door. Every shadow in the stairwell seemed to hold breath. Every corner felt watched. By the time she reached her door, her hands shook too badly to fit the key on the first try.

When it finally clicked open, she bolted the lock behind her and pressed her back to the door, breathing hard. The silence that greeted her was not comfort—it was suspicious. The kind of silence that could be broken by the wrong kind of knock.

Her phone buzzed. A message from Lucas.

Are you okay? Did you get out safe?

She didn't answer.

Instead, she walked to the bathroom sink, splashed cold water on her face, and stared at her reflection.

"You're not crazy," she whispered. "But you're definitely being hunted."

She dried her face and grabbed the burner phone Jasmine had given her weeks ago, hidden in a hollow book beneath her nightstand. She dialed the encrypted number.

Jasmine answered on the second ring. "You're calling me before coffee. This must be serious."

"I found something," Emily said. "More than I should've."

"Whisper Protocol?"

"Yes. And the authorization file was signed by Ryan Mercer."

Jasmine let out a low whistle. "Well, that's going to be a fun conversation."

"I need your help again. There's a trail here, but it's fractured. Can you dig deeper into Subject 07?"

"Send me the ID. I'll run it through the scrubbed archives and black-market mirrors. Give me a few hours."

Emily paused. "Jasmine... someone was in the archive room while I was there. I didn't see them. But they were close."

Jasmine's voice dropped to a whisper. "Then be ready for them to get closer."

Later that morning, the ER was chaos.

Multiple ambulances had arrived within minutes of each other—overdose, crash, chest pains. Emily pushed through the fog of exhaustion and adrenaline, snapping on gloves, barking orders, doing what she did best: saving lives.

Lucas passed her once, their eyes locking across the trauma bay. He didn't speak, but the look in his eyes told her everything. He hadn't slept either. They were both pretending things were normal in a world that had tipped off its axis.

As the dust began to settle, Emily ducked into the break room to check her messages. A new encrypted file from Jasmine was waiting.

Subject 07 – Confirmed Identity Match Name: Andrew Harlow Relation: Father of Dr. Emily Carter

Emily's breath stopped. Her father—Andrew Harlow. Memories flooded back: him humming while cooking breakfast, his laugh echoing through the house. The warm calloused hand that used to hold hers on walks. Her chest ached with a grief freshly sharpened by betrayal.

She read it again. And again.

The patient who'd been experimented on. Terminated. Her father.

Her hands went numb, the phone nearly slipping from her grip.

Emily didn't remember walking to Lucas's office. But suddenly she was there, shutting the door behind her and leaning against it like it was the only thing holding her up.

Lucas looked up from a patient chart, alarm flashing in his expression. "Emily?"

She handed him the phone. "Read it."

He did. Slowly. Then he looked at her, eyes wide. "Jesus... Emily—"

"My father wasn't in a coma. He died of cardiac arrest in a hospital across the state."

Lucas stood. "Are you saying they moved him here? Without permission?"

"I'm saying they faked everything. His death. The records. And used him in a trial that killed him again."

Lucas reached for her, but she stepped back.

"I don't even know who to trust anymore." Her voice cracked. "First Ryan. Now this?"

He nodded, grounding his voice. "Then we find the truth. Together."

She didn't resist when he wrapped his arms around her.

Her body shook with silent sobs, tension bleeding out of her like a tourniquet had finally loosened. For a long time, they stayed that way. No words. Just breath and warmth.

That night, Emily sat at her kitchen table, a single desk lamp casting long shadows. The tick of the old wall clock was too loud. The scent of coffee grounds lingered faintly from that morning, now stale. Her fingers trembled as she unfolded the letter, the weight of her father's handwriting already anchoring her breath.

She opened her father's sealed military file, one she'd requested months ago but never had the courage to read.

Inside was a letter.

Emily,If you're reading this, I'm gone. Not just gone—erased. There are things I knew, things I saw, that people wanted buried. But you have your mother's strength. And I believe you'll find your way.

Trust your instincts. But not your memories. Some of them aren't yours.Love, Dad

Emily sat frozen, tears blurring the words. Not hers? What did that mean?

Her phone buzzed.

Another message from Jasmine.

Archive footage recovered. Sending now.

The video loaded—a dim corridor, a figure entering the archive room shortly after Emily had left.

It was Ryan Mercer. Emily's breath caught. A thousand thoughts screamed at once—accusation, disbelief, fear. But louder than all of them was one piercing realization: the man she'd looked up to might have been the one who pulled the strings from the start.

Chapter 15 – A Knock at Midnight

Emily's hands trembled as she poured hot water into her chipped ceramic mug, the peppermint tea steeping in slow, swirling clouds. The apartment was quiet, but her mind wasn't. It hadn't been since the footage.

Ryan Mercer. The man she trusted. The man who welcomed her into this hospital.

Her father's name still echoed in her head.

Andrew Harlow. Subject 07. Terminated.

She hadn't told anyone about the file. Not even Lucas. Not yet. Not until she could breathe again without the weight of betrayal crushing her chest. Her chest felt heavy, her limbs leaden. A silent scream of disbelief echoed inside her as she stared at the tea swirling in the cup. She saw her father's eyes in her memory—alive, warm—and now framed in black-and-white stills labeled "terminated."

A knock startled her.

She spun, heart hammering, nearly dropping the mug. Another knock—calm, rhythmic. Too late for neighbors. Too early for dawn.

She inched to the peephole.

Ryan Mercer stood outside, dressed in black slacks and a gray trench coat, rain misted across his shoulders like static. He held no umbrella. Just a neutral expression and a manila envelope tucked under one arm.

Emily froze, breath catching. Should she call Lucas? Her fingers hovered over the burner phone. But then her anger surged hotter than fear.

She unlocked the door.

"Dr. Carter," he said smoothly. "May I come in?"

"Why? So you can lie to my face too?"

He gave a tight smile. "I think it's time for transparency. For both of us."

Reluctantly, she stepped back.

He entered with measured confidence, scanning the apartment like a man familiar with control. Emily crossed her arms.

"Cut the act. I saw the video."

Ryan tilted his head. "I suspected you might."

"So? What was your plan? Wait until I disappeared too?"

"Emily," he said, placing the envelope on her kitchen counter, "you're standing in the middle of a chessboard. You don't even realize it yet."

She stepped forward, eyes blazing. "My father was Subject 07. He died twice because of *your* protocol. So tell me—how many more names are buried under your little secrets?"

A flicker of genuine emotion crossed his face—regret? Fear? She couldn't tell.

"I didn't authorize his termination," Ryan said, voice low. "I tried to stop it."

"Then who did?"

He looked at the envelope. "Everything you need is in there. But know this: if you keep digging, they'll come for you. Not to silence you—but to use you."

"Use me?"

He turned to leave. "You'll understand. Soon."

The door clicked shut behind him.

Emily locked it. Bolted it. Then tore open the envelope.

Inside: black-and-white surveillance stills. One showed her father strapped to a gurney. Another—blurry—captured a woman in surgical scrubs with the nametag *J. Mercer.*

Her hands froze. Jasmine? No. That couldn't be right.

Her heart pounded, confusion tangled with betrayal. Had Jasmine known all along? Or had she been another pawn in this web?

Before she could process more, another knock hit the door.

Not rhythmic. Not calm.

Pounding.

She grabbed the burner phone and pressed speed dial. It rang twice.

"Emily?" Lucas's voice.

"Someone's at my door. I think I made a mistake."

"Stay on the line—I'm already on my way."

She didn't move. Her breath caught as the doorknob twitched. Then—silence.

Lucas arrived ten minutes later, breathless, his hair damp from the rain.

He searched the hallway—empty. "They're gone."

Emily let him in and collapsed onto the couch. Lucas sat beside her, concern tightening his features.

"What happened?"

She told him everything—the file, the footage, Ryan's visit, the envelope.

When she mentioned the picture of Jasmine, Lucas's eyes widened. "She said she left the agency years ago."

"I don't know what to believe anymore."

Lucas reached out, brushing her hand. "Believe this: you're not alone. I'm not leaving."

Emily looked up at him. In that moment, her defenses cracked. She leaned forward, and Lucas met her halfway.

Their kiss wasn't soft. It was desperate—months of tension, grief, fear, and longing igniting at once. Lucas's hands cupped her face as her fingers tangled in his hair. Every movement was a release, a cry for connection. She let herself feel—for once, completely.

He guided her gently back, lips trailing down her jaw, her throat. She gasped, pulling him closer, wanting to forget the world outside the door. But as his hand slid beneath her shirt, a noise outside snapped her back.

A footstep. Then silence.

Emily froze. Lucas sat up, alert.

They both listened.

Nothing.

"I'll check it," he whispered.

"No—wait."

Emily grabbed the envelope again. A small slip of paper had fallen out.

A torn page. Coordinates. A handwritten word across the top:

Renascent.

Lucas looked at it, frowning. "That's a research site. Outside city limits. Decommissioned."

"Not anymore," Emily said. Her voice steady now. Sharpened.

Another knock at the door.

She stood. Lucas reached for her arm, but she shook her head.

This time, she didn't flinch.

She opened the door.

And gasped.

Chapter 16 – Shadows Return

Jasmine stood in the doorway, drenched and trembling. Her hospital ID was gone. Her hair clung to her cheeks like wet string. In one hand, she clutched a flash drive. In the other, a crimson-streaked cloth.

Emily's breath caught in her throat. Her stomach dropped. "Jasmine?"

Lucas stepped protectively beside her.

Jasmine's voice was barely above a whisper. "They know I helped your father."

Emily pulled her inside without another word. Lucas locked the door behind them and drew the curtains tighter. The atmosphere inside thickened with unspoken questions and the growing scent of rain-soaked fear.

Jasmine swayed as she stood in the middle of the room, then collapsed to her knees. The flash drive clattered to the floor.

"You're bleeding," Emily said, kneeling beside her.

"Not mine," Jasmine said hoarsely. "I ran. I had to. They're covering their tracks. Starting with anyone who still knew the name *Renascent*."

Lucas picked up the flash drive and examined it. "What's on here?"

"Enough to burn them to the ground."

Emily's eyes locked on Jasmine's. "You told me you were out. That you were done with all of it."

Jasmine looked ashamed. "I tried. But you don't leave *Renascent*. Not really."

Lucas moved to the window, peeking through the blinds. "We need to move. Now. If they tracked her here—"

"I know they did," Jasmine cut in. "One of them had my photo. One of *us* gave it to them."

Emily froze. "Someone from St. Theresa's?"

Jasmine nodded. "Ryan Mercer's not who he pretends to be."

Emily didn't flinch. "I know. He came here tonight."

Jasmine's expression crumpled. "Then we don't have much time."

Lightning flashed outside. The power flickered. Lucas grabbed his bag and tossed Emily hers.

Jasmine handed her a wrinkled envelope. "This has the map to the Renascent facility. There's a way in through the east service tunnel. But we need to go before sunrise."

Emily nodded and turned to her bedroom, stuffing clothes and the burner phone into her bag. She paused when her hand brushed against a worn leather-bound notebook—the same one her father had written in after long hospital shifts.

She hesitated, fingers lingering on the weathered spine, then slid it into her backpack.

Lucas met her at the door. "We'll take the back stairs. I'll hotwire something untraceable."

They moved quickly, Jasmine limping slightly, clutching her side. The wind howled outside as they stepped into the alley behind the building. A red glint appeared for an instant on the brick wall near Emily's head.

Lucas yanked her back just in time. A second red dot danced on the wall before vanishing.

"Sniper," he whispered. "Go!"

They sprinted down the alley, cutting through puddles and garbage bins. The wind stung their faces, but adrenaline drowned everything else. Emily's chest burned, her legs aching, but she didn't slow.

They found an old delivery van with an expired plate. Lucas popped the lock and hotwired it within seconds.

"Get in!"

The engine sputtered to life. Emily helped Jasmine into the back, then climbed in beside Lucas.

Rain battered the windshield as they sped through the dark city streets.

The van rumbled along a dirt path flanked by pine trees and barbed-wire fencing. Ahead, under the dying beam of the headlights, loomed the concrete carcass of the Renascent facility.

Emily's heart pounded harder with every mile they covered. She stared out at the silhouette of the building—weathered, cracked, and abandoned in appearance. But something about the darkness felt intentional, too symmetrical.

Lucas parked behind a thicket. The engine clicked as it cooled.

"Jasmine," he said, "you sure about that tunnel?"

She nodded. "East wall. Near the drainage pit."

They slung their bags over their shoulders. Lucas handed Emily a flashlight and a compact pistol from his glove compartment. She stared at it.

"You trust me with this?"

"I trust you more than anyone else right now."

Emily exhaled and took it. The weight settled in her palm like gravity itself.

The walk to the wall was silent. Every rustle in the brush sounded like footsteps. Every gust of wind, a whisper.

They found the grate where Jasmine said it would be—half-buried under dirt and vines.

Lucas wrenched it open with a grunt. A tunnel stretched into darkness, slick with moisture and the stench of mold.

Emily looked at him. "We go together."

He offered her a faint smile. "Right behind you."

She crawled in first, the narrow walls closing in. The smell hit her throat like a punch—chemical rot and something faintly metallic. She kept moving.

Behind her, Lucas grunted as he dragged Jasmine through. "Tunnel gets tighter ahead," she warned.

Minutes felt like hours. Finally, a faint light shimmered ahead.

They emerged into a corridor lined with abandoned carts and broken tech. Emily's boots crunched glass.

A red LED light blinked on the wall. Active security.

"Doesn't look so decommissioned to me," Lucas muttered.

Jasmine leaned heavily on the wall. "We're close. Just ahead, the observation deck. That's where they kept your father."

Emily's breath hitched.

Lucas stepped closer, touching her elbow gently. "You okay?"

"No."

She turned and faced him. The dim emergency light haloed his face. "But I need to know the truth."

Lucas cupped her face. "We'll find it. Together."

She leaned into him, lips brushing his, slow and deliberate. A kiss not born of desperation this time—but of strength. Of choosing something real amid everything false.

Their foreheads touched. Her fingers curled around the collar of his jacket, drawing him closer. A warmth spread through her despite the chill. In the quiet, his thumb brushed her cheek—a silent promise in the dark.

Jasmine's whisper broke the moment. "Footsteps."

They turned. Shadows flickered down the corridor.

Lucas raised his pistol. Emily backed to the wall.

Then, a voice echoed.

"Dr. Carter. We've been expecting you."

Chapter 17 – Through the Veil

The voice echoed like a cold wind against concrete.

"Dr. Carter. We've been expecting you."

Emily froze, her fingers tightening around the pistol Lucas had given her. Lucas shifted closer to her side, eyes scanning the hallway for the source. Jasmine pressed her back against the wall, her breath ragged.

The footsteps approached—steady, measured. Then a figure stepped into view beneath the emergency lighting. A man in a lab coat. Not disheveled. Not afraid. Calm. Too calm.

His hair was silvered, skin pale under the sterile glow. An ID badge swung from his chest: Dr. Charles Virelli. Below that, stamped in faded ink, was the old Renascent logo.

"Who are you?" Lucas demanded, gun raised.

Virelli smiled as if they were guests arriving for dinner. "The better question is: Why are you here?"

Emily stepped forward. Her heart pounded, a memory flashing in her mind—her father standing by the kitchen window, talking about someone named Virelli in hushed tones. "You knew my father."

He dipped his chin, acknowledging. "Dr. Jonathan Carter. One of the brightest minds in our program."

Jasmine shuddered beside her.

Emily steadied her voice. "Where is he?"

Virelli's eyes glittered. "He left behind more than just data." He gestured toward a side corridor. "Come. If you truly want answers, you'll find them here."

Lucas stepped in front of Emily. "And if we don't?"

"Then the people hunting you will. But not for answers. For containment."

Lucas didn't lower his gun, but he nodded. "We go together."

They moved as a unit, Emily's hand grazing Lucas's as they walked. Jasmine limped along, face pale. The hallways twisted like veins through the building—each one colder, darker. The sense of being watched pressed in from all sides.

Finally, Virelli opened a biometric lock. The heavy door groaned as it slid open, revealing a lab frozen in time.

Monitors blinked. Papers covered the desks. On one screen, a static image of a brain scan remained locked in place, annotated with notes in a handwriting Emily knew by heart.

Her father's.

She stumbled forward, drawn to the terminal.

"His last session," Virelli said. "Before everything fell apart."

Emily scrolled through the logs. Timestamps. Code. Descriptions of neurological spikes. Sudden memory recoveries.

And then—

Subject 17: Evidence of transfer. External memory imprint detected. Emotional resonance confirmed.

Lucas leaned over her shoulder. "Is that what they were doing here? Transferring memories?"

Virelli nodded. "Not just memories. Consciousness. Identity. He called it the Veil. The line between self and memory. He wanted to save people from degenerative diseases. What we built... others wanted to weaponize."

Emily turned to him. "Where's my father now?"

Virelli stepped back. "His mind didn't survive the final transfer. But..." He motioned to the screen again. "He left something in the system. A residual trace. We think he tried to encode himself into the prototype core. Subject 17."

Jasmine gasped. "You didn't—You used a patient?"

Virelli's smile faltered. "We used a volunteer. One who believed in the cause."

Lucas turned to Emily. "Is this what your father wanted?"

Emily blinked back the sting of tears. "He wanted to stop suffering. He never wanted this."

From behind, a sharp clang.

Lucas turned, gun raised. "That wasn't the building settling."

"Security," Jasmine said, voice dry. "They're here."

Emily's gaze locked on the core interface. Her fingers trembled. "Can I access him? What's left of him?"

Virelli nodded. "If you connect through the neural port."

Lucas grabbed her arm. "Emily, no—"

She placed her free hand on his chest. "Lucas, I have to. I need to know. Please."

Their eyes held for a long second. He cupped her cheek, thumb grazing her skin. "Come back to me."

"I will."

She slipped into the chair, connected the leads. The hum of electricity buzzed against her skin. The world narrowed.

Darkness.

Then—a voice. Familiar. Gentle.

Emily?

Her chest tightened. "Dad?"

I tried to warn you. It's not safe.

"Where are you?"

A part of me... here. But the rest is gone. They twisted it. You have to finish what I started.

A memory surfaced—her father's arms around her as a child, whispering bedtime stories about stars that never died.

The image of a terminal filled her mind. Codes. A shutdown sequence.

Outside, gunfire.

Lucas yelled. Jasmine screamed.

Emily's hands flew across the keyboard. A klaxon began to blare.

System shutdown initiated.

Virelli's eyes widened. "What have you done?"

"I gave him peace," Emily said.

Flashing lights. Explosions in the corridor.

Lucas pulled Emily to her feet. "We need to go. Now."

As they ran, he grabbed her hand. "I thought I lost you."

"You never will," she gasped, leaning against him.

They ran. Jasmine beside them. Virelli stayed behind, hands outstretched toward the dying screens.

Thank you, the voice whispered, fading.

They disappeared into the tunnel as fire engulfed the lab behind them.

Chapter 18 – Beneath the Surface

They ran until the only sound was their breath echoing in the narrow maintenance tunnel. Emily's lungs burned, her legs trembling with every step. She forced herself forward, each stride haunted by the echo of her father's voice inside the machine—by the memory of his lullabies and the static sorrow in his goodbye. Behind them, the Renascent facility smoldered, a dying monster collapsing into ash.

Lucas guided them through turns and junctions as if he'd memorized every inch of the blueprints. Jasmine followed close behind, clutching her ribs. The silence between them was thick with everything they hadn't said yet.

They emerged into a maintenance bay behind an old research annex, tucked away behind locked steel doors and decades of disuse. Lucas pried open the emergency hatch with a wrench and motioned them inside. The room was dim and sterile, abandoned long ago.

Emily collapsed onto a bench, brushing sweat-soaked hair from her forehead. Her fingers still tingled from the neural interface.

Lucas knelt in front of her. "Are you okay?"

She nodded, but her voice cracked. "He was still in there. My father. Not all of him, but enough."

Jasmine slumped against the wall. "That facility wasn't just hiding tech. It was hiding trauma."

Lucas turned to her. "How long were you there?"

She hesitated. "Months. They kept me drugged at first. Then they tried to make me work. I escaped when I realized what Subject 17 really was."

Emily's voice was soft. "Did you know he volunteered?"

Jasmine nodded, eyes misting. "He thought he was helping humanity. Not becoming a digital ghost."

Lucas sat beside Emily, his shoulder brushing hers. "You shut it all down. You gave him peace."

Emily looked at him, really looked. His face was streaked with grime, his eyes red—but the way he looked at her held no fear, only unspoken affection.

She leaned into him, drawing comfort from his warmth. "I'm scared. Not of dying. But of what I'll become if we don't stop this."

Lucas cupped her jaw gently. "Then we stop it together."

Their lips met, soft at first—an unspoken agreement, a tether anchoring them to something human amid the chaos. It wasn't like their first kiss, desperate and stolen in a moment of panic. This was slower, deeper—born of choice, not crisis. The kiss deepened, their hands finding each other's faces, arms. Emily clutched his shirt, pulling him closer. For a brief moment, the world fell away.

They broke apart, breathless. Jasmine had turned away, giving them privacy.

Emily whispered, "This doesn't feel wrong."

Lucas smiled, brushing a thumb over her cheek. "That's because it's not."

The moment ended as Jasmine cleared her throat. "Sorry to ruin the vibe, but we've got movement on the surface grid. Someone's sweeping the area. Military pattern."

Lucas was instantly on his feet. "We have to move. There's a secondary tunnel network under the annex. It leads to the marina. We can lose them in the water."

Emily stood, adrenaline returning. "Then let's go."

They descended into a lower tunnel lit by flickering emergency lights. Water dripped from corroded pipes overhead. The air grew damper, colder, like stepping into the belly of some forgotten machine.

They moved quickly, Lucas leading with flashlight drawn, Jasmine covering the rear. Emily's thoughts spun—about her father, the voice in the system, the line between humanity and machine.

Suddenly, a voice crackled through a nearby vent shaft.

"Target acquired. Tunnel C. Close and converge."

Lucas muttered, "Damn it, they've triangulated us." His voice was tight with urgency, the walls seeming to vibrate with approaching boots and the metallic clatter of weapons being readied.

Gunfire erupted down the corridor. The walls lit up with muzzle flashes. Jasmine returned fire, yelling for them to run.

Emily and Lucas sprinted, ducking into a rusted side shaft. The air reeked of oil and mold. Behind them, Jasmine shouted something—then fell silent.

Emily turned, panicked. "Jasmine!" Her eyes caught the brief glimpse of Jasmine's silhouette in the dim tunnel, framed by sparks and gunfire—then swallowed by shadow.

Lucas caught her arm. "We can't go back. Not yet."

Tears welled in Emily's eyes. "We don't leave people behind."

Lucas didn't argue. He just pulled her forward. "We find another way around."

The tunnel forked. Lucas chose the right path. After fifty feet, they stumbled into a storage room with cracked concrete and a narrow ladder leading up.

He looked at her. "This gets us above ground. Marina's two blocks north from here."

She nodded, wiping her face. "Let's finish what they started."

They climbed together into the foggy dawn. Emily paused at the top, glancing back once into the tunnel's darkness, silently vowing that Jasmine's sacrifice wouldn't be for nothing.

Chapter 19 – Through the Fog

Emily and Lucas emerged into the sharp breath of morning. The marina lay before them, cloaked in a gauzy veil of fog that blurred lines and softened the chaos of the night. The horizon was a faint smear of light, and the salt-laced air clung to their skin. The world felt muted, suspended, as though even time had paused to catch its breath.

Lucas crouched behind a storage shed and surveyed the perimeter. Patrol drones skimmed the skies in a lazy pattern overhead, their searchlights barely piercing the fog. A guttural hum of distant engines echoed off the water.

"We need to keep low," he said. "There's an old fisherman's wharf on the northern edge. If we can get there, I know someone with a boat. Quiet engine. No transponder."

Emily nodded, her fingers still trembling. Her mind raced, half anchored in the moment, half haunted by Jasmine's last scream. The image of her silhouette disappearing into the tunnel firestorm was carved behind her eyes.

They slipped between the boathouses, moving quickly, Lucas leading. The ground was slick with dew and scattered seaweed, and every creak of wood beneath their feet sounded like thunder.

At the edge of a half-sunken vessel, they ducked behind a stack of lobster traps. Emily caught her breath. "Do you think she made it? Jasmine?"

Lucas didn't answer right away. His eyes scanned the dockyard, his jaw tense. "I want to believe she did."

A moment passed. Then he turned to her, his voice softer. "But even if she didn't, she gave us a chance to stop all of this."

Emily swallowed hard. She hated how helpless she felt. She hated that grief was becoming a permanent fixture.

They crossed a crumbling gangway and entered an abandoned boathouse. The scent of brine and engine oil filled the stale air. Inside, the light was dim, filtering in through broken panes.

Lucas pulled a tarp off an old speedboat tucked behind crates. "It still floats. Not fast, but fast enough. I'll check the tank."

Emily wandered to the window, brushing dust from the glass. She stared into the fog, searching for something—hope, perhaps.

"You okay?" Lucas asked.

She turned slowly. "I don't know how to mourn someone who might still be alive."

Lucas approached her, his movements careful. "We're not done. And you haven't lost her. Not if there's still a chance."

She met his gaze. There was no bravado in his tone, only quiet conviction. In that moment, she didn't feel like the broken girl who once ran from everything. She felt present. Alive. Seen.

She reached for him, and he closed the distance. Their kiss was slow, deep, not rushed by danger but grounded in the storm of everything they'd survived. Fingers tangled in hair and fabric, pulling each other close, not just for comfort but for something more primal—the need to feel human again.

They didn't undress, didn't rush. Just lips, hands, breath. The intimacy was in the connection, not the exposure. And when they finally parted, foreheads resting together, there was peace in the stillness.

Emily whispered against his neck, "I don't want to lose you too."

"Then don't," Lucas murmured. "Not now."

Outside, the world had begun to stir.

A crackle of static buzzed from the corner. Emily's head snapped toward the sound. Lucas pulled a small emergency radio from a supply crate. It had sprung to life on its own.

The signal hissed and spat. A garbled voice bled through the static.

"...Echo-7...contact...contain...Subject...J..."

Emily lunged for the device. "Run it again. Boost the gain."

Lucas adjusted the dial. The voice returned, fractured but clearer.

"...north pier...holding...Subject...J17...coordinates...encrypted...Butterfly sings...Emily, if you're hearing this.."

Emily froze. "That was Jasmine. 'Butterfly sings' was our code. She made it up back in college when she got caught sneaking into the archives. It meant she was in deep and needed help."

Lucas stared at the radio. "They didn't kill her. They captured her."

She stood. The fear was gone. In its place: fury. "Then we get her back."

Suddenly, a shadow darkened the window. Lucas spun, drawing his sidearm. The door creaked open.

A figure stepped through, hooded, soaked in fog.

Emily raised a wrench from the floor. "Don't move."

The figure lifted their hands slowly. "Easy. I'm not with them."

Lucas narrowed his eyes. "Then who are you with?"

The figure pulled back their hood. It was a woman—mid-40s, scar along her jaw, eyes sharp and weather-worn.

"Name's Calla. I used to run darkwater routes for the resistance. Jasmine sent me. Before they took her. Said if anything went sideways, I'd find you here."

Emily blinked. "You know Jasmine?"

"Well enough to trust her instincts. She talked about you more than once—how you'd be the one to keep fighting when everyone else gave up."

Lucas lowered his weapon slightly. "What's the plan?"

Calla stepped inside, shutting the door. "I've got a boat and a back channel through the old storm drains that feed into the bay. But we need to move. The Renascent will be crawling all over this district in minutes."

Lucas glanced at Emily, then nodded.

Emily paused at the door, casting one last glance at the fog outside. Her voice was quiet but fierce. "Jasmine bought us time. We're going to make it count."

Together, they stepped into the fog, toward the northern pier—and into whatever waited for them next.

Chapter 20 – The Edge of the Storm

The storm drains reeked of rust and brine. Emily crouched low as they moved through the narrow tunnel, her boots sloshing through ankle-deep water. Above them, the marina was a world away, but every clang of a pipe or distant echo kept her pulse hammering.

Lucas led the way, flashlight beam cutting across graffiti-scarred walls. Calla brought up the rear, her footsteps nearly soundless, her eyes constantly flicking behind them. The weight of the silence was oppressive.

"Almost there," Lucas murmured, glancing at a hand-drawn map. "Two more bends. Then a maintenance hatch. That should lead us under the pier."

Emily nodded but said nothing. Her focus narrowed to the sound of her own breath, the thrum of adrenaline. Jasmine was alive. And close.

The tunnel curved sharply, and a soft blue glow filtered in from ahead. Lucas motioned for them to stop. He crouched at the corner, peering around it.

Emily crept beside him. Through the grate, they could see a chamber lit by flickering overhead lights. A rusted catwalk ringed a holding area, where steel crates and old equipment formed makeshift barriers. In the center, a reinforced door pulsed with an electronic lock.

Lucas whispered, "That's a Renascent staging chamber. Must've converted this from an old maintenance hub."

Calla exhaled slowly. "Your sister's in there. But if they've fortified it, they'll have guards. Maybe surveillance."

Emily clenched her jaw. "We can't turn back now."

Lucas nodded. "Follow me. Quiet as ghosts."

They ascended a ladder bolted to the wall. The hatch opened with a hiss, revealing a rusted utility space above. Lucas helped Emily up, then Calla. They crept through shadows, weaving around broken machinery and dim emergency lights.

Emily's heart pounded harder with every step. At the far end of the chamber, the reinforced door loomed. A keypad blinked beside it. No guards visible, but the tension in the air was thick.

Lucas examined the keypad. "Standard biometric lock. I might be able to spoof it."

Calla pulled a tool from her belt. "I've got a scrambler. Bought us into more than one vault back in the day."

As they worked, Emily stepped back, scanning the room. Her gaze landed on a small camera tucked into a beam overhead. Its lens was cracked—recently, from the looks of it. And there were scratches on the floor near the door, like someone had been dragged.

Her gut twisted. "They moved her recently. Maybe even during the chaos above."

Lucas cursed under his breath. "We're running out of time."

The lock clicked. The door shuddered, then slid open.

Emily burst through, Lucas at her side. The room inside was stark. A cot, a sink, surveillance screens. And Jasmine.

She sat hunched in the corner, arms wrapped around her knees. Her face was gaunt, lips cracked, eyes rimmed with exhaustion—but they snapped open the moment the door opened.

"Emily?"

Emily rushed forward, pulling her into a fierce embrace. Jasmine's body shook with relief.

"You're alive," Emily whispered. "You're really alive."

Jasmine clung to her. "They kept asking about you. About Dad. They know so much."

Lucas moved to the monitors. "We've got maybe five minutes before they notice this breach."

Calla stood watch at the door, weapon drawn. Her voice was steady, but her eyes scanned the shadows. "We need to move. Now."

Jasmine's voice dropped. "There's more. I found files—deep in their system. They're planning something. A mass trial. A purge. Not just us. The whole city."

Emily's blood went cold. "You have proof?"

Jasmine nodded and pulled a small drive from her boot. "Encrypted. But it's all there. Names. Timelines."

Lucas took it, his hands momentarily trembling as he slotted the drive into his portable terminal. "We need to get this out. Broadcast it. Make it public."

Suddenly, an alarm shrieked.

Calla snarled, "They're here."

Lucas grabbed Jasmine's arm. Emily took the lead.

They ran.

Through the corridor. Down the ladder. Into the tunnels.

Gunfire rang out behind them. A bolt sizzled past Emily's ear, scorching the wall. Lucas fired back, dropping one of the enforcers. Calla hurled a flash charge, filling the tunnel with smoke.

They sprinted through the water, lungs burning. Emily's foot slipped on algae-slick metal, but Lucas caught her before she fell, steadying her with one arm. Their eyes met for a heartbeat.

"I've got you," he said, the words more than reassurance.

At the final bend, light shimmered ahead—moonlight on open water.

The storm drain spat them out beneath the pier. Calla's boat bobbed nearby, engine humming.

Lucas shoved Jasmine aboard. Emily followed. Calla jumped in last and hit the throttle.

As the boat peeled away from the pier, bullets kicked up water behind them.

Emily held Jasmine close, heart pounding. She looked to Lucas, who was already scanning the drive.

His voice was hushed. "It's worse than we thought. They're going after the Resistance leadership next. They've mapped everything."

Calla steered them into the fog. "We've got a safehouse upriver. A clean signal. We'll get this out. Then we burn every last shadow they hide behind."

Emily reached for Lucas's hand. He laced his fingers through hers.

"I'm not losing either of you," she said. "Not now."

Lucas looked at her, eyes fierce. "Then let's make it count."

The fog swallowed them, but their course was clear.

Whatever came next, they would face it together—hearts aligned, truths in hand, and nothing left to fear.

Epilogue – After the Storm

The river had always held a quiet kind of magic. In the early morning light, mist drifted over the surface like whispered promises. Emily stood at the edge of the dock behind the safehouse, Jasmine beside her, wrapped in a borrowed sweater several sizes too big.

"I never thought I'd breathe free air again," Jasmine said softly, watching a pair of birds skim the water's edge.

Emily smiled, brushing a strand of hair from her sister's cheek. "You held on. That's what matters."

Behind them, the safehouse was quiet. Calla was inside, on her third cup of coffee, coordinating with Resistance cells across the city. Lucas had fallen asleep on the couch hours ago, laptop still open beside him, the data Jasmine recovered finally decrypted and transmitted to trusted media outlets.

The storm had broken.

The broadcasts had hit the public feeds before dawn—files exposing Renascent's abuses, its planned trials, the corruption at the highest levels. The city was already erupting with protests, internal resignations, and a rising wave of defiance.

Jasmine turned to Emily, her voice tentative. "So what happens now?"

Emily took a deep breath, letting the river's calm steady her. "We rebuild. We help others come out of the dark, like we did."

A soft sound behind them made her turn. Lucas stood in the doorway, arms crossed, a faint smile tugging at the corner of his mouth. His shirt was wrinkled, and there was a pillow crease on his cheek—but his eyes lit up when they met hers.

"You're up early," he said.

Emily arched a brow. "Says the guy who worked all night."

He stepped closer, glancing toward Jasmine. "Hey. You holding up okay?"

Jasmine gave him a tired but grateful nod. "Better, thanks to you both."

She turned and wandered back inside, leaving Lucas and Emily alone on the dock.

The silence between them was comfortable now, like the hush after a song that lingered in your chest.

Lucas looked out over the river. "You ever think we'd make it to the other side of all this?"

"I wasn't sure," Emily admitted. "But I knew I'd fight for it."

He slid his hand into hers. "You didn't just fight, Emily. You led. You healed. And you gave me a reason to believe again."

She blinked, emotion catching her by surprise. "I didn't do it alone."

"No," he said, tugging her closer. "You didn't."

She rested her head against his shoulder, letting herself feel it—everything she had tried so long to lock away. The ache, the hope, the quiet joy of not having to carry it all by herself.

Lucas tilted his head toward hers. "So what do we do now?"

Emily smiled. "Live. Maybe... breathe. Kiss when the mood strikes."

His laugh was low and warm. "You always did have the best plans."

She reached up, brushing her fingers along his jaw. "And you, Dr. Hayes, are overdue for some peace."

He kissed her gently, and the world slowed. No alarms, no gunfire, no shadows lurking in the corners—just the soft lapping of water and the steady thrum of something new beginning.

In the distance, a siren echoed—not of danger, but of change.

Together, hand in hand, they stepped back toward the house. Toward the future. Toward a life earned not in spite of the pain, but because of the strength it forged.

The halls were quiet now.

But their hearts were loud with promise.

Acknowledgments

This story could not have come to life without the encouragement, inspiration, and quiet strength of those who walk beside me, even through the fog.

To the readers who believe in second chances, emotional truths, and the kind of love that doesn't flinch in the face of darkness—thank you for turning the pages with open hearts. You are the reason stories like this matter.

To all the frontline heroes—doctors, nurses, first responders—who carry the weight of others' pain while still holding on to their own humanity, this book is a tribute to your quiet resilience and relentless compassion.

To the storytellers who came before me, and the mentors and friends who lifted my voice when I couldn't quite find it—your belief helped me keep going.

And finally, to anyone who's ever fought their way back from heartbreak, fear, or loss—I see you. This story is for you.

With gratitude and hope,

Trevor Jensen

About the Author

Trevor Jensen is a storyteller at heart, drawn to the pulse-pounding edges where danger meets redemption, and where love blooms even in the darkest corridors. With a passion for emotionally rich narratives and characters who fight for second chances, he writes stories that blend suspense, heartache, and healing into unforgettable journeys.

When he's not immersed in writing, Trevor enjoys exploring coastal towns, sipping too much coffee, and imagining the secret stories whispered behind closed hospital doors and city skylines.

Heartbeat in the Halls is one of many stories born from his fascination with human resilience—and the quiet, powerful courage it takes to open your heart again.

To see more books and audiobooks by Trevor, please visit his coming-soon web site at http://www.TrevorJensenBooks.com